THE DRAGON'S TRUE MATE

THE DRAGON KINGS OF FIRE AND ICE BOOK 5

AMELIA SHAW

CHAPTER
ONE

Lucian

I staggered out of the hall, away from my brother's wedding and the woman he'd taken as his bride. His fated mate.

Sarah and Dymitri had been perfect together from the very start. From the moment they met, I'd been able to sense the intensity of the feelings Dymitri had for her.

Desperately, I'd hoped it would be the same for me and my mate. Marienne had said it would be, but that wasn't the case. I'd felt nothing except sympathy for Nadia when we found her injured and unconscious.

When she woke up, there had been none of the intense feelings I'd been promised. No passion. No quivering desire. No dragon rearing his possessive head.

The lack of those feelings had sent me into a rage unlike any other. I'd felt so hurt and betrayed. So disappointed. But I'd gotten through it and hoped to one day find my own mate. Perhaps a servant in the castle or one of the women in town.

But no... today I'd met my own fated mate. It was another

human woman. Just like my brother. And my dragon was bursting to be free.

I erupted through the door of the grand ballroom, my gut tightening to the point of having to run bent over.

"Hold it together," I muttered to myself, not sure that I could.

Running for the entrance of the castle, I passed through the foyer that had only recently been patched up. Dymitri and I had done enormous damage to the once-grand colored glass windows when I'd flown into a rage over Nadia not being my mate. Not my finest hour. Nor my dragon's.

I burst through the front doors, feeling the cold blast of our icy winter breeze on my face.

Reveling in the sensation of the crisp chill, I deeply breathed in the air.

Calm down, calm down.

My dragon was furious at me for running away, snarling and snapping inside my mind. He wanted to go back and find his mate, but I couldn't.

I was teetering on the verge of being out of control and if I returned to the wedding party, I'd destroy everything in sight. There was no hope of containing my dragon any longer.

He needed to be free.

My dragon rose up inside of me as I stripped off my suit jacket and threw it on the ground. Wings sprouted from my back, and my skin transformed into the leathery scales of my shifter form.

I closed my eyes and let my mind go as mist swirled up around me, and I became my dragon.

When I opened my eyes, the world around me looked different. But the feelings inside of me weren't.

My mate was here, and Marienne had been right after all. My fated mate was human, and a sister to Sarah. But it hadn't been her tiny, younger sister Nadia as we'd all thought. Instead, my mate was her older sister. The gorgeous, generously curvy Katerina, with dark, curly hair and a sexy smile that made my skin catch fire.

Not to mention her ass... *oh my God.* My cock ached just thinking about her curves.

I leaped into the air, beating my wings against the sky.

Everything that I'd been told about fated mates was true. My dragon was uncontrollable in his need, my human side having no chance of dominance. My heart was thudding against my chest with the power of a steaming locomotive. Lust poured through me, all for a stranger. A woman who would never understand my world or our customs.

I'd never been good enough for my father to accept, nor any woman I'd known in the past. Why would this gorgeous human want me now?

Memories of my anger and hurt from past traumas poured through me like molten lava, eating away at any hope I had for my future. None of this made any sense to me, and in my growing fury, I couldn't see a way around the problem except to gain altitude and fly away.

I soared higher and higher, until I couldn't move my wings any longer. Until I was afraid I might fall from the sky if I didn't stop ascending.

Soaring back down to a lower altitude, I continued until I was far away from my half-brother's kingdom. Until sunshine heated my wings in place of winter chill, and my skin ached from the rapid change in temperature.

There was another kingdom ahead of me, with a huge castle perched high above the surrounding lands and villages. I could only hope it was Stavrok and Lucy's castle. I'd never been to visit them in their home but had met the royal couple when they'd visited Damon and Cass.

I glanced back the way I'd come, weak now from hunger and fatigue. I'd never make it back. Not tonight. Not without a rest. I used the last of my strength to fly down and land on a high balcony attached to the castle and there I collapsed against a railing.

I let my dragon go and shifted back to human, my chest heaving with the strain and my legs trembling in their attempts to hold me up. An older male servant hurried out onto the balcony to greet me, his gaze narrowing as my human body replaced my dragon.

"Let me get you a robe, sir," he said with a polite incline of his head, then stepped inside once more.

I sighed with relief at the confirmation I was in the right place. That was definitely a royal servant, so this had to be Stavrok's palace. None of the servants in the winter palace treated a stranger so well.

The man returned with a warm robe that I slipped on gratefully. "Thank you."

Then he handed me a glass of water, which I downed immediately. The coolness flowed over my aching throat, soothing it, making me moan with gratitude.

"Can I help you, sir?" he inquired. "Are you here to see King Stavrok?"

I nodded, though it wasn't entirely true. I'd ended up here purely by accident. "Could you tell Stavrok and Lucy that I'm here? My name is Lucian. He'll know who I am."

The servant bowed and walked away. I managed to put down the glass of water and tie up the robe just as an older man dressed in fine clothes stepped out onto the balcony.

"Lucian, sir, please follow me."

"Thank you."

I followed the man, who was likely the steward, into the castle, marveling at the richness of the carpet underfoot and the beautiful paintings that lined the halls.

What a difference it made when the king in charge of his

kingdom actually looked after his wealth. Unlike my father, who'd been a tyrant king and let his people and his castle fall to ruin.

He'd been the worst of men.

You're not him, and you're far away from his memories. Let it go.

I gazed about Stavrok's castle and briefly indulged myself in the fantasy of what life might have been like if I'd grown up as the bastard son of this king. Raised in this home, or within the castle's walls. Perhaps then I wouldn't be such a fucking mess.

The steward stopped in front of a large, wooden door. "King Stavrok is waiting for you in here, sir. He's aware of your arrival."

Wonderful. Hopefully he doesn't kick me straight back out again. It wasn't like he knew me well.

The man opened the door and held it open for me to head inside. I took a deep breath and moved forward. Part of me had expected an office or a sitting room, but instead I was staring down the length of a grand dining hall with an impressively long wooden table.

At the head of the table sat King Stavrok, food laid out before him and a glass of red wine in hand. When he saw me, he grinned and waved a hand toward the seat across from him. "Lucian, take a seat. What brings you here to my humble home? Isn't your brother getting married today? That's the rumor I heard, at least."

King Stavrok was a huge man, and even seated, cast an imposing figure.

"You heard correctly," I mumbled as I sat down in my robe, feeling more naked than before. "The ceremony took place earlier and I expect the reception is well underway as we speak, in fact."

"Please, help yourself." Stavrok gestured to the feast before him.

I poured myself a glass of wine and picked up a bread roll, my gut still churning with the accumulation of stress. I wasn't very hungry, but I wasn't going to turn down the king's generosity.

"So, Lucian, tell me why you aren't at the wedding." The king tilted his head to the side, no doubt curious as to why I would leave such a joyous occasion and travel so far away.

I wanted to tell him it was none of his business. That he could stick his nose elsewhere and leave me be.

But I'd shown up at his home unannounced, and owed him an explanation. He had a human mate from the other side of the veil, his wife, Lucy, so perhaps he'd offer me some advice.

Certainly, my brother, Dymitri, would have tried to help me. However, I had no intention of burdening him further. Not on his wedding day, of all days. Just seeing me flee the ceremony had probably left him worried enough.

I needed a sounding board. "My fated mate is at the ceremony."

Stavrok's brows rose. "I repeat then, why aren't you there?" He chuckled.

I saw nothing amusing about the situation but instead of answering immediately, I took a bite of my roll and a sip of the wine. Then another. I hadn't realized how much I needed sustenance.

I inhaled deeply to regain some control, then released my breath slowly. "I'd just come to terms with the fact that I wasn't going to have a fated mate. That the sorceress, Marienne, had been wrong about my future. After all, she'd been so sure it was Nadia. She's the—"

"The other woman we rescued from that human hell hole." King Stavrok shuddered. "I remember."

"I thought Marienne's vision had been wrong, and prepared myself for never finding my true mate. I'd made peace with that."

Stavrok grinned at me as though he knew what I was about to say. "Marienne hasn't been wrong about our fated mates. Not yet, anyway. She was the reason I found Lucy."

"Oh, I didn't know that." And I hadn't. So, Marienne had been a royal matchmaker from the beginning? Somehow, that made this story even more credible now.

"I didn't mean to interrupt," Stavrok said, pouring us both some more wine. "Go on."

I blew out a breath. "Well, it turns out Sarah has another sister and the moment I saw her... everything fell into place. I wanted her. I still want her. And the only thing I could do to keep myself from taking her on the spot—or destroying everything around me—was to flee." I paused, the shame of my lack of self-control washing over me. "I felt like a monster, getting lost in that lust."

The king's expression softened. "You're a better man than me. I kidnapped Lucy from her home. I had no control."

My jaw dropped. "You..." *He kidnapped her*?

He nodded. "Yes. Literally picked her up and flew her home."

I didn't know Stavrok well, but I knew men. And he was serious.

"Did she forgive you?" I couldn't imagine Katerina letting me pick her up and carry her to my bedroom.

Stavrok cackled out a laugh. "Of course. Eventually. But tell me more about your mate. Why don't you believe she'd forgive you for letting your dragon have his head? After all, it's the most natural instinct we have."

I reached for some fruit, picking apart the grapes and orange. "Katerina might not want me at all. I'm not exactly the easiest to love."

A fact that had gotten drilled into me at an early age. I'd spent so much of my young life being told I wasn't worthy. Why would that change now? What would she see that everyone else missed?

The answer was nothing. Once she got to know me, she'd come to the same conclusion. Having her and then losing her might kill me.

Stavrok sighed then motioned for a butler who had been

patiently waiting nearby to come closer. "A bottle of whiskey, I think."

"Yes, my king." The butler bowed and left in a hurry.

"Here's what you're going to do," King Stavrok said. "You're going to calm down and get out of this spiral of doom you've placed yourself in. Then you'll remember this woman is your fated mate. She was created *specifically* for you. Her soul is the other half of yours. She is what will complete you, and she is going to love all sides of you. Even the ones that are difficult or not really that loveable."

"How do you—"

He gave me a sharp look that shut me up. "Because we all go through those thoughts, and we all have difficult pieces to love. No one is perfect, Lucian."

I pressed my lips together tightly, wanting to argue. Stavrok didn't know me, and he couldn't imagine what my life had been like.

But I kept my thoughts to myself. He was a king, and I was a bastard son. Even though he was allowing me to sit at his table and drink his wine, we weren't on the same level.

The butler returned with a bottle of golden whiskey. Stavrok poured me a glass and placed it right in front of me. "Once you've collected yourself and rested a little, go back to the wedding and be with your mate. Show her the depth of your feelings for her."

"She's human. What if she doesn't understand? They don't feel the pull the same way we do." Or so I'd heard.

Stavrok laughed. "I guarantee you, she will. It might not be the exact same sensation, as she doesn't have the dragon inside of her. Her heart will know, though. It will beat faster when you're around. Her gut will twist whenever you're near. Her body will have the pull of extreme desire, and her heart will war with her head until she gives in. Sound familiar?"

"Yes." So similar. Perhaps humans weren't as strange as I'd originally thought.

"She is going to love you." He sounded confident. "But it will take a lot longer if you keep running from her every time her presence makes you a bit uncomfortable."

A bit uncomfortable is an understatement.

The moment I'd laid eyes on her, my cock was at full attention and every part of me had been eager to explore every inch of her curvy figure. No other woman compared. I'd never been set ablaze in such a way before in my life. If I couldn't do something about that discomfort soon, I might explode.

"Next time, I'll be more prepared," I said, much calmer than I felt. I couldn't guarantee that, but I'd pretend for the moment. "If nothing else, it won't be such a big surprise."

"I need to go and speak to my wife. Shall I leave you with your thoughts?" Stavrok asked.

No. My thoughts frightened me. All the same, I said, "Yes." I picked up my glass of whiskey. I'd intruded on his hospitality long enough.

"I'm always happy to help," Stavrok said in a soft voice. "I'm glad you felt enough trust in me to come here."

I appreciated him saying that more than I could express. He was treating me as an equal when I was only King Damon's bastard brother.

"Thank you for your assistance." Despite the fear creeping through me, I knew what I had to do, and I had a plan of action to take.

Stavrok left me, and I took the time to finish my whiskey, letting the warmth soothe my inner dragon. My strength began to return, and a new determination stirred within me. A determination to face my fear, and seek out my fated mate.

Once I was able, I transformed into my dragon and flew back to Damon's castle. It was indeed, a long way, though I did not ascend so high this time and the air was better for breathing. When I arrived, I found a private place to change back into human form.

I'd obviously missed the ceremony, and felt terrible for that. But Dymitri would understand, I felt sure, as would Sarah. I'd seen it in my brother's eyes just before I fled the castle, and he would explain what had happened to Sarah. Everyone would understand, except for *her*. My one true mate.

By the end of the night, I would make it up to her. I did not want to be the mate who ran away.

I gathered all the courage I had and made my way to the hall where the reception was still underway. My heart was pounding like a battering ram, but after my long flights, I had enough control over my dragon to walk into the room without feeling like I was going to shift.

My gaze settled on my mate sitting across the room, and a piece of me I thought long dead sprang to life once more.

TWO

Katerina

Even though we were in a castle, my sister's wedding was small and simple, which was fitting for her. The fact that she was marrying a guy she'd just met wasn't very typical, but I tried not to judge her too harshly for that.

It was easy to understand her falling in love so quickly, especially considering her new husband was one of the men who'd rescued her and Nadia from hell.

I wouldn't be following that path any time soon, of course. Love at first sight just wasn't my style. But I was glad at least one of us was getting an epic, whirlwind romance worthy of a romance novel. As long as he loved her and took good care of her, he'd stay off my shit list. I'd give this Dymitri guy the benefit of the doubt, especially when I saw the way they looked at each other.

Dymitri. Even his name sounded like something from a fairytale. I tried to keep my jealousy at bay, not wanting to be bitter.

That wasn't right. Instead, I focused on the joy I felt for my sister as she walked down the aisle. She glowed as she gazed into the eyes of her new husband.

As Sarah and Dymitri exchanged their vows, a strong yearning tugged at my heart. That part of me that didn't want to be alone anymore. I knew nothing came easy. As a chubby girl, I understood that I had to work a lot harder to stand out in a crowd full of size-zero wannabe supermodels.

Easy would be a nice change.

I gazed through the small crowd of mostly strangers and noted the original best man still missing from the group. I'd caught one glimpse of him earlier, and then he'd disappeared. Strange. And even stranger was how much I'd felt his absence. I tried to shake off the feeling and refocus my attention on Sarah. This was *her* day.

Tears were shed as the bride and groom were officially pronounced husband and wife. Up next was the reception where I fully intended on hiding behind a drink and pretending I belonged. Something about the party guests seemed unique. Not bad, just different, but I couldn't quite put my finger on what it was.

Everything about the wedding was different, in fact. Sarah was being married in a picturesque mountain village, over which the castle loomed like a medieval dream. I had so many questions, and yet I didn't want to ask, not wanting the magic of the day destroyed.

And then, speaking of magic, *he* walked back into the room. As soon as the best man stepped through the door, it was like a spell had been cast over my body. My legs quivered. Actually quivered! Something I only thought happened in fiction.

I clung to my glass of wine, suddenly fearful I wasn't going to be able to stand much longer. My knees got wobbly and there was a tingle between my legs I hadn't felt in too long to count. I swallowed hard, unable to drag my eyes away from him. My whole body flushed with heat, and I finally looked down to try and get some control back over my physical reaction to his presence.

Holy hell! All that from *looking* at one of the most majestic men to ever walk the earth.

The best man. Now I was sad I'd only caught a glance earlier. Clearly, I'd missed out on quite the specimen. Long, dark hair that gracefully fell to his shoulders. And he was so tall! Even from a distance, he towered over everyone and everything. A broad frame, too. Those arms... that chest... I'd kill to have them wrapped around me.

I'd kill to wrap parts of me around him too, for that matter. He was imposing enough I wouldn't feel like I was squishing a bug.

A gentle hand on my arm startled me out of my trance. My sister, the happy bride, smiled at me.

"Let's go say hi," Sarah said, nodding her head toward Tall, Dark and Dangerous.

More heat flushed through me, this time primarily in my cheeks. "What? To him? Why?"

"He's my husband's brother, and family should meet family, right?" She winked suddenly. "Besides, I think you two would hit it off."

Smashingly well, I hope.

I cleared my throat. "Good point."

Sarah slipped her arm in the crook of my elbow, and we walked across the room together. Each step toward him was like floating on a cloud. No way was my sister about to introduce me to the most gorgeous guy on the planet. No way!

Then, the next thing I knew, I was standing in front of him and gazing up into his deep, soulful, dark eyes. *Hot damn...*

"Lucian," Sarah said and gestured between us. "This is my other sister, Katerina."

He gazed down at me with such intensity, I lost my footing

and stumbled just a tiny bit. Toward him, I should add—much to my embarrassment. Lucian caught me before I face planted into his rock-hard abs. I didn't know they were rock-hard for sure, but based on what I'd seen it was easy to assume. His whole body was probably chiseled from stone.

"Heels," I said, struggling to find an excuse for my clumsiness. "They're big. Long. Tall."

Oh God, I was mortified, because immediately my mind went to other things that were big, long, and tall. In my four-inch heels, I barely made it to his shoulder. He was just so fucking tall in comparison, and I was all for it. But I doubted a guy like that would be into a woman like *me*.

"You should be careful with those," he said, his voice a low rumble that caused my insides to churn with desire.

I laughed, awkward and too loud. "Just need more practice with this pair. I bought them for the wedding." The conversation was tanking fast. "Anyway, it was really nice to meet you..."

I turned back toward my sister and shot her a warning look that suggested she better not stop me from leaving.

"Kat!" Sarah insisted, clearly not caring or not catching what I was trying to communicate. I walked past her, and she turned her attention to Lucian. "We'll be right back."

I found an empty table to sit at. The music for the dancing had started, and the loud thumping of the bass was a nice distraction from my thoughts, but also made it impossible to think clearly.

No, if I were being honest, Lucian made it impossible to think. Simply having him in the same room turned my brain into a pile of glittery, hopeful mush. Story of my life... I see an attractive guy and let lust cloud my logic, which always resulted in heartbreak.

"What is wrong with you?" Sarah gasped out, standing over me with her hands on her hips. "Katerina... you bolted before you even got a chance to actually *talk*!"

"Clearly, the conversation wasn't too riveting," I snapped, pressing the palm of my hand to my forehead. "My shoes, of all things… I had to talk about those. He's going to think I'm some kind of shallow ditz!"

"No, he's not."

"No, who's not?" our other sister, Nadia, asked, joining us at the table. "What did I miss?"

I groaned. "My humiliation with Tall, Dark and Dangerous."

"Lucian?" Nadia asked, looking over at him.

We all did, and I noticed he was staring intently back… at me. He wore a deep frown that seemed almost concerned. For me? I gave him a small wave, and that brought a smile to his face. It was such a beautiful sight to behold that I had a difficult time looking away.

"Yes," I said at last. "Lucian. Sarah thought I should meet him since he's our new brother-in-law's brother, or whatever. Then I lost my footing and almost fell into him, and it spiraled from there."

"It did not," Sarah insisted. "It was not that bad!"

She didn't understand. At all. For someone like her, it'd be cute. For me… I shook my head. "I'll talk to him later when I'm not so…" I made a vague gesture around me, hoping that explained everything. No such luck.

Nadia reached out and grabbed my hand. "I'm with Sarah on this one. Go and say hello to him. Talk. Dance!"

"Oh, yes, dancing! That's a great idea." Sarah pulled on my arm to try to get me out of my seat. "Then you'll be a little more relaxed. Small talk is always hard to get past, so maybe just skip it. I don't think Lucian is into that anyway."

Why were they being so pushy?

I looked back toward him, and he gave me a small wave, his eyebrows raised in an inviting fashion.

"Is there something I don't know that you're not telling me?"

"No," they both said at once, making it even more suspicious.

After a brief moment of silence and one shared glance, Sarah spoke. "Dymitri seemed to think you and Lucian would hit it off well, and I agree. In fact, I heard he's nervous to talk to you."

"Seriously?" I didn't buy it. A guy like that wouldn't get nervous.

She nodded. "He's... not exactly a people person. Kind of rough around the edges. I know you haven't had a lot of luck with guys, but I wouldn't suggest you two talk if I thought it was a bad idea."

"I feel really good about it too," Nadia added. "Neither of us would lie to you or set you up for failure."

They'd conspired against me! I couldn't believe it.

That being said, Lucian was... wow. And I did trust them. They'd never let me down before. I just wish the set-up didn't have to seem so desperate. Guys never found that attractive. But if he truly wanted to talk to me, then maybe I'd judged him too quickly.

"All right, I'll ask him to dance," I said. For the moment, I had my nerve, and I wouldn't let my head talk me out of it.

Sarah grinned and Nadia clapped.

I took a few steps forward, and Lucian's eyes seemed to light up. He moved toward me, meeting me halfway in front of the buffet table where the night's feast was spread.

"You seem to have practiced walking," he teased.

I shook the joke off, my legs going weak again. I wouldn't stumble any more. I would show him how confident and sexy I could be. "What can I say? I'm a fast learner." I paused. "Would you like to—"

"I was just about to get something to eat," he said. "I took a long journey unexpectedly and it'd be nice to replenish that spent energy."

"Oh." So much for my sisters steering me in the right direction.

"And I'd like you to join me," he added. "Because after..."

"After?" I asked, gazing up into his eyes. Immediately, I was lost.

He smirked. "After, I'm sure I'll have plenty of energy."

Doubt tried to creep into my head. This guy was way too hot for me. But I shoved it aside. Trust. I knew I had to trust my instincts about him. I couldn't say how I was so certain of that fact, but it felt right. I'd never get anywhere if I always played it safe.

"Sounds perfect. I'm pretty hungry too, to be honest."

He walked me to the table, and we loaded up our plates. I followed my instinct there too, not going crazy, but not sticking to only the veggies from the salad tray either. The way my heart was continuing to race in his presence, he wasn't the only one who had to stock up on energy!

Soon, we sat down at a table together and tucked into our plates.

"You went on a journey," I said. "Everything okay? I saw you missed the ceremony."

His gaze never left me, instead wandering over my body more than once. "Everything is perfect. Now, I mean. It was a personal problem that needed attending to."

"Sounds like you found the resolution to your problem then," I said. "I'm glad. I noticed you were missing."

"You did?" He seemed surprised.

I nodded. "I only saw you for a second, but I put two and two together when you rushed out. Something was up."

"You're observant," he said. "And kindhearted."

I felt the heat return to my face. "When I want to be."

"May I always inspire you to keep being so," he murmured. He cleared his throat. "Are you enjoying your time in my half-brother's castle?"

"How could I not? It's a castle!"

I cleared my plate a lot faster than was probably lady-like, but Lucian seemed to be on pace right along with me. Almost like we both wanted to finish our food and get to whatever came next.

"Ready to dance?" I asked. "Feel replenished?"

"Very much so." He offered his hand to me, and the second our fingers touched, an electric shock ran through my body.

I heard a sharp intake of breath from him, and then his arm slid around my waist and he led me through a waltz as a slow song conveniently started playing. My hips and chest pressed against his. God... I had no resistance in me when it came to this man.

"Confession," I said softly, just barely loud enough for him to hear over the music. "These aren't actually new shoes. You just... have a way of making me forget how to function."

He leaned his mouth to my ear. "I'm relieved. I was worried I'd scared you off, or that you thought I was disgusting."

"No woman in her right mind would think you're disgusting." I giggled at the preposterous thought.

"You'd be surprised." He pressed his cheek against mine. "But I don't care what other women think. You're the only one whose opinion matters."

My heart began to beat even faster and my whole body grew hot. "You're still talking about me, right? I'm not being punked, am I?"

"I don't know what that means but yes, this is a two-person conversation. No one else is around. It's only us." He took in a heavy breath. "I'd love to kiss you. Would that put your mind at ease?"

"It certainly wouldn't hurt," I managed.

He wants to kiss me? Someone pinch me, because I have to be dreaming.

Then his lips were against mine, firm and sweet, in a kiss that started out chaste and pure but quickly morphed into more. I opened my mouth and teased his tongue with mine. It was only a small taste of what I wanted to give him. Passion pulsed through me, hot and insistent. I had to have him. Logic be damned.

"I have a room," he said, his voice rough with need.

I nodded, growing wet just thinking about being in private with him. "Lead the way."

He took me by the hand and led me from the grand ballroom. I glanced around to see if my sisters were still watching, wondering what they'd think if they caught me. Sarah was too busy with her new husband, and Nadia was nowhere nearby. I shook my head. They'd lose their minds once I told them. A one-night stand was the last thing anyone expected from *me*. I'd always been into feeling secure with a commitment before taking things to such a level of intimacy.

But Lucian felt different. I might never get a chance with such a god of a man again. Seriously, it wasn't every day someone so incredibly sexy wanted *me*. If I declined his invitation, I knew I'd regret it.

He led me up the stairs, stopping halfway up to push me against the wall and claim another kiss. I was more than happy to oblige him. His lips were warm, his arms were strong. Tingles flooded my body. We couldn't get to his bedroom fast enough as far as I was concerned.

We hit a landing and started running down the hallway. I picked up the hem of my dress so I wouldn't trip on it, and laughed at his enthusiasm. We stopped outside a room, he opened the door, then tugged me inside.

As soon as the door was closed, I pushed off his suit jacket. His hands moved to slide the straps of my dress down and in seconds, he had the zipper at the back moving as well.

This guy was an expert at undressing women, that was for sure.

I ripped open his button-down shirt, buttons popping off and rolling onto the floor. Underneath that fabric was a body made for a billboard. His abdomen was so defined, it could have been made of stone. It had to be. There was no way a human man could be so chiseled and rock-hard. And that wasn't the only thing rock-hard.

I could feel the power of his erection as he pressed against me. I was wet in anticipation and clawing at his pants to break him loose. When his cock was finally freed, the sight of his length made me shiver.

He was hard and long, the head red and engorged. Wanting *me*. Needing *me*.

I had to have him inside me.

Now.

I dragged Lucian over to the bed and crawled backwards over the mattress. He moved over me, nibbling up and down my torso. His kisses were everywhere, starting between my breasts, then he moved down my abdomen to my mound.

I gasped out as he pushed apart my legs, then his tongue teased me in the most sensitive of places and I moaned the loudest I've ever moaned in my life. Normally, I'd have been embarrassed if I made a sound like that, but God, it felt so fucking good, I didn't care who heard.

I twisted in the silken sheets, grabbing at his hair to anchor myself. He didn't stop, flicking over my throbbing clit with his lips and tongue until I was screaming for him.

"Get inside me, please," I begged. "Stop being a tease!"

His head came up and he said with a smirk, "If that's what my lady wishes."

"Yes!" *Of course, it fucking is!*

Lucian didn't wait. He crawled up between my legs, spread me even further apart with one of his thighs, and readied his cock at my entrance. Then he plunged hard, sinking his cock into my channel. I cried out at the welcome invasion. My back arched involuntarily, my body receiving his fierce invasion as if it had been waiting for him my whole life.

I dug my nails into his back, holding him tightly to me as he withdrew slightly, then filled me again. We were ravenous with one another, each giving as good as the other. Lucian began to move faster, harder, claiming me like his life depended on it. Every thrust sent a powerful wave of pleasure through my body, driving me toward climax at a level I'd never experienced before.

And even when I tipped right over the edge and screamed and shuddered as the release took me, he wasn't done.

He showered my face and body with kisses, withdrawing so that he could suck on my hard nipples and twirl them with his tongue. I moaned again, unsure of how much more I could stand.

When he grabbed my ass and entered me again, I sobbed with relief. Nothing had ever felt so good before. So right. He pushed me to orgasm yet again, only this time when I began to climax, he released a might roar and came deep inside me at the same time I lost control and arched up and into him, screaming.

My belly rippled as he shuddered within me, my body shivered beneath his, and it was minutes before I came back to earth from the most amazing climax of my life.

"Oh. My. God," I gasped out, breathing hard.

He let out a satisfied groan, then rolled onto his side, facing me.

"I... is it okay if I stay for a while?" I asked. "I know that's presumptuous but I don't think my legs will work right now."

There was no way I was jumping up and leaving if I didn't have to. My belly was still tight and aching, and the need to be close to this man had only amplified.

Lucian gazed over at me, smiling, only... were those tears in his eyes? No, I had to be imagining that. It must only be the afterglow of an epic fuck.

He kissed my forehead. "Stay as long as you'd like. I have no intention of letting you go."

I raised an eyebrow, but who was I to argue? He wrapped me in his arms, and, surrounded by his warmth, I drifted off to sleep.

CHAPTER

THREE

Lucian

I slept long and deep, possibly the most satisfying sleep I'd ever had in my life. Never before had I felt so content, so at peace. For the first time ever, all the missing pieces in my heart seemed to be there, whole and complete.

All of it felt like a dream, too surreal to be true. And I would have doubted the whole night had occurred until I rolled over and Katerina's luscious, warm body pressed into mine.

I didn't want to let her out of my sight for fear she might disappear. She could have snuck away in the middle of the night but chose to stay. That had to mean something.

Gazing down at her beautiful face and with her dark curls lying across my pillow, my inner dragon stirred. Once I'd returned to the wedding for the reception, I had somehow found the strength to stay in control of the beast lurking within. *Stay calm. Soon enough.*

I'd kept the dragon quiet so Katerina wouldn't see that side of me too soon. When Nadia had witnessed me transform, she'd run away and taken Sarah with her. We'd almost lost both of them that night. Humans weren't used to seeing any sort of magic, let alone mythical creatures. In her world, I was nothing more than a myth... and a monster.

Upon waking and seeing her still there in my bed, I relaxed, letting my guard down.

Katerina shifted in her sleep, her lush body moving closer to mine as if by instinct. The fresh touch of her skin against mine ignited a fire in my soul.

It's her. She's the one. The other half. I'm complete.

My stomach churned with the immediate change within my body. I tensed and recited calming words inside my head.

Stay in control. Stay calm. It's okay to be excited, but I have to be careful. I don't want to scare her away.

I squeezed my eyes shut, trying to focus on the war raging inside my mind as two sides of me fought for dominance.

We're bonded now. We're one now. My dragon's celebration grew as Katerina's eyes opened and her gaze landed on my naked chest.

"Morning," she said, and an adorable blush spread across her cheeks.

"Morning," I murmured back, pushing a lock of hair away from her eyes. "How did you sleep?"

"Wonderfully." She let out a blissful-sounding sigh. "I'll be honest. I don't do this kind of thing, like, ever."

I gazed down at her curiously, unsure how to interpret her statement. "Do what kind of thing, exactly?"

"Fall into bed with someone I just met." Her voice got awfully quiet. "Totally worth every second."

A grin spread across my face. "Definitely worth the leap of faith on my part, as well." If only she knew how much of a leap it was on my end. My dragon stirred at the memory of becoming one. How much that alone meant...

Calm down!

"I'm sorry, I didn't mean to stay all night," she said. "But I was so tired and so content."

I frowned. "Why would you leave?"

"Isn't that how these things work?" she asked.

These things… did she mean a one-night stand? "I wasn't intending for this to be the only time we—"

Her beautiful eyes grew wide, though I couldn't tell if it was excitement or surprise that colored her expression. "No?"

"No."

"That's a relief, because I was kind of hoping for seconds this morning. Or is that selfish and forward of me to presume?" She placed a hand on my upper thigh and, at the feel of her exploring fingertips, that's when I lost all control.

I groaned as my body started to respond to my shifter's elation. "E-excuse me, I…"

I rolled out of the bed and staggered toward the door. I had to leave the room before I shifted in front of her.

When she saw my dragon for the first time, I wanted it to be after I'd explained more about the world she was now going to be a part of. Throwing her straight into the thick of it without any pre-warning would be far too overwhelming.

My dragon had other plans, though.

"Lucian, are you okay?" She sat up in bed, holding the sheets up to cover her chest. "Maybe I should leave. We can talk later… or if this is your way of kicking me out so that my feelings aren't hurt…"

"No!" My voice came out in a growl. "I want you to stay. I want to talk. I want…" *A whole life with you.* That's what I wanted to say. But I couldn't get the damn words past my shifting throat. "Just…a few… minutes…"

I reached the door but before I could stagger through it, the change began to happen.

Fuuuck!

I fought it hard but lost. My body grew bigger, my eyesight shifted, and wings unfurled from my back.

In moments, I was in my dragon form. He demanded a celebration for finding our mate, and I'd fought him back for too long.

I beat my wings to stabilize myself before setting my clawed feet on the ground.

Oh, no. Please, Katerina, don't freak out.

My dragon form took up the space between the bed and the door. Luckily there was more than enough room, as all the rooms in the castle were designed with our transformation in mind.

I turned to look at my mate, horror curling around my mind. What was she going to say?

Katerina sat on the bed, frozen. Her jaw slowly dropped, and her eyes grew wide. "Oh... wow..."

If that was her whole reaction, then perhaps things wouldn't be so bad after all.

But it seemed she was in shock. And the initial effect wore off more rapidly than I thought it would. Suddenly, she let out a blood-curdling scream. I automatically roared in response, the pitch of her voice piercing my ears. Not my finest moment.

"Oh my God! Ohmygod, ohmygod, ohmygod!" She covered her ears, squeezed her eyes shut and threw the blankets over her head. "Don't eat me! I am not food! Ohmygod."

I needed to speak to her and there was only one way. I gathered all of my strength and forced my shifter back inside. Slowly, too slowly, I became a man once more.

"Katerina? No! I'm not going to—"

A small squeak escaped her lips as she sat bolt upright again and pulled the sheets down once more. Her face was bright red and flustered. "You talk? Are you a demon? You have to be some kind of unholy monster from Hell to talk! To change shape! You were just… a man and then a dragon… ohmygod…" She started to breathe, heavy and fast.

"Katerina, I'm still Lucian. I'm a—"

"No! Stop! I'm not going to fall for it! I've seen this movie! A million times! It never ends well." She whimpered. "Oh, God… please tell me this is all a dream. None of this is real. All a dream. All. A. Dream."

My heart felt as if it broke in half. Pain tore through my chest as the intensity of her fear amplified. Of course, she was frightened. Why wouldn't she be? To her, I was a predator searching for its next meal.

The question was, should I run?

Yes. In fact, the further I distanced myself from her, the better. She sounded on the verge of hyperventilation, and someone else in the castle must have heard the scream and my roar. They might even be on their way already.

I'd distressed her, my presence terrifying her. One of her sisters could provide her with the care and comfort she'd need, and I would be far away, unable to cause her more harm. Yes, that was definitely the best course of action. Then she wouldn't be able to watch me fall apart from her rejection. She didn't even try to listen…

I let my dragon loose, allowing him to fly up into my body once more, the panic within my heart settling as my beast took over. I flew out the nearest window, glass crashing to the ground as I took to the sky. I'd already caused plenty of damage to Damon's castle fighting with Dymitri. What was one more window?

The wind kissed my scales, and I barreled toward the forest—toward home. Not the castle that Damon insisted was now my home, but my true one. The one in exile. That's where I belonged, in the land of banishment where my asshole father had put me.

Why did I think I could ever leave? Why did I think I could make a home in the castle and have a happily ever after?

I didn't deserve anything like that.

How could I have been so stupid?

I wanted to rip the world apart. To destroy the trees, the buildings, whatever got in my way. Wanted to but didn't. Enough of my humanity remained to remind my dragon that setting the world ablaze would do more damage than good. A mournful cry left my lungs as I soared into the clouds. There, I could wallow in my misery as much as I wanted.

She was supposed to understand. Her heart was supposed to respond to mine and give her the compassion and grace to accept the dragon inside me. It hadn't, probably because I wasn't worthy of her love. At least I'd had one night with her. I'd rewind and replay the night over and over again for the rest of my life.

The cool air calmed me some. I felt more human than dragon again. I almost turned back toward the castle, so I could transform once more and try to comfort her now that my rational and more logical side had returned. Perhaps we could talk. She might still listen...

Then I remembered the large, terrified eyes staring up at me, pleading with me not to eat her. The way she'd nearly gone into shock. Leaving her alone was still the best option. She didn't need my presence complicating things further. One of her sisters might have more success at getting her to understand, then maybe I could take over from there.

I just had to wait things out. Steer clear so I couldn't cause her any more pain or angst.

I found the small shack I'd called home through my formative years and landed in the small clearing near the front stoop. There, I changed back into a human and made my way inside.

"It'll be fine," I said to myself as I walked into the kitchen to splash some water onto my face. I groaned. "Who am I kidding?

It's not going to be fine. She hates me. My fated mate hates me and thinks I'm a monster."

It had been all over her face. Not just fear, but loathing as well. She'd called me a *demon*! That was how she made sense of my shifting ability, jumping to the worst possible conclusion.

Maybe she was right. A monster's blood did course through my veins. My father had been a terrible creature. He'd banished Dymitri and me when we were children, leaving us for dead. He'd preyed on the people who relied on him for their survival. Everything he did was for his own selfish gain, no matter the cost or who got hurt along the way.

As much as I wanted to be a better man—as much as my brother told me I *could* be one—I wasn't a fool. I was doomed to repeat my father's mistakes.

There's a reason the phrase, "Like father, like son" exists. Perhaps Dymitri lucked out and most of his nature came from our mother. I clearly hadn't, though. I'd seen parts of my father in my soul in the past. The fact I couldn't control my dragon as easily as others could was another sign. I desperately wanted to *not* be like him. But I was his flesh and blood, and it showed.

If I didn't mate, then I couldn't have my own children, and that meant I wouldn't keep the cycle of his insanity going.

Katerina deserved someone who was able to love her to the fullest and provide the best future possible. I wasn't capable of either of those things. I wasn't worthy to even try. Failing her would kill me far faster than her rejection.

No, I would spend the rest of my days alone, living on the memory of our one beautiful night together. At least one of us might then have a chance at happiness.

FOUR

Katerina

O*h my God! Oh... my... God.*

Did I just see what I thought I saw? One moment, Lucian was his tall, handsome, sexy self, staggering around the room naked like he had a stomach ache. The next, his skin melted into scales and his long limbs became wings growing from his body.

He turned into some kind of dragon, right in front of my eyes! I said demon, but a dragon felt a lot more accurate some-how. How was that even possible? There was no way dragons could be real. They belonged in fairytales and movies, not real life!

I didn't wait for anyone to come to me. I threw on my dress and underwear from the night before and ran from the room with my shoes in hand. Not the leisurely post-sex morning walk I'd planned on taking, that was for sure.

I'd been hoping for a more subtle approach to leaving Lucian's room. One that didn't scream the "bridesmaid just fucked the best man!" cliche to the whole damn castle. Instead, I'd screamed my lungs out, and probably woke everyone up.

There was a definite lack of commotion in response, which to me seemed odd. A scream and an inhuman roar should have had everyone scrambling to help. At the very least, spark an investigative curiosity. I didn't run into a single soul until I was halfway down the grand stairway and met my youngest sister coming up toward me.

I must have looked half-crazy, because Nadia suddenly picked up her pace and ran to me. "Kat!" She flung her arms around me. "Are you okay? I thought I heard you scream but wasn't sure you needed help."

"Why would you think... *oh!*" She'd thought I was screaming as part of my lovemaking with Lucian. "Took you long enough," I said, breathing heavily.

Nadia squeezed me harder. "I was on the other side of the castle eating breakfast. It's kind of a huge place, if you hadn't noticed. Are you okay?"

"I'm not hurt," I said. Not physically anyway, I figured. Just my pride. Tears pooled in my eyes. "I'm not okay, though."

She urged me to sit down on the steps. "What happened?"

That was when Sarah arrived. She stood at the top of the stairs with her new husband beside her, took one look at me and her shoulders sank. "Oh, Kat..."

I gazed up at her and shook my head. "Go back to your honeymoon." I could see from her disheveled hair and swollen lips that I'd interrupted something.

"Dymitri will understand." She gave him a pointed look. He nodded and whispered something into her ear before disappearing back along the hallway. Sarah walked down the stairs and sat on my other side. Both of my sisters held me close and I felt comforted and slightly less disconnected in their presence. "Tell us everything."

"I took your advice and danced with Lucian," I said. That seemed the easiest place to start. Maybe if I put it all together from the beginning, it might make more sense to me as well. Everything about coming to the castle felt like a dream. "We hit it off, like you said we would."

"That's wonderful!" Sarah's eyes grew wide with excitement.

I bit my lip and shifted uncomfortably. "We hit it off *really* well, and I stayed the night in his room."

"Ooh-la-la!" Nadia teased.

I shot her a glare. "Our morning started great. We woke up and were kind of canoodling in bed. Then he started acting funny. Like he was sick. I thought maybe he was faking it so he could get rid of me. That he'd gotten what he wanted from me and everything else had just been a line."

I want you to stay. I want to talk. I want... What had been that third thing he wanted but never got to say? His eyes had been so sincere, his words so pure.

"It wasn't a line," Sarah said. "Kat, he—"

"I'm not finished," I said stiffly. "So, he's pacing madly around the room, trying to get me to understand he's honestly not well. Just as I'm about to believe him, he... he..." The memory of his transformation and the way he'd spoken to me in that rough growl sent a shiver down my spine. "You're not going to believe this, but he turned into a monster."

"A dragon," Nadia said.

"Right, it looked like a—" I frowned. "Wait a second, you *knew?*"

She pressed her lips together tightly, her eyes avoiding mine. "We met before the wedding, and he might have done the same thing in front of me, too." She hurriedly added, "Not after having sex with him. I never touched him, I promise! But he has a tendency to get overly emotional and then—"

"Changes into a dragon!" Sarah finished. "Lucian is passionate, and he's passionate about *you*, Kat."

I held up my hands. "You *both* knew?"

"Yes," they said together, both quiet after.

I took in a slow breath, trying to keep my rage at bay. "Why didn't you tell me all of this *before* I met him! Before we... we..." Had the most incredible sex of my life. Oh, goodness. I'd never been loved so thoroughly. "That one detail changes so much!"

"Would you have believed us?" Sarah asked. "I certainly didn't believe it until I saw it with my own eyes."

Nadia nodded slowly. "It's a lot to take in. I had the same reaction you did, Katerina. I ran away!"

"We both did, because it was almost too much to handle," Sarah continued. "But then I saw the softer side. The man behind the beast. Lucian is still in there. You have to look past the scales and the rough exterior and then you'll realize nothing about him has actually changed. That's what I did with Dymitri."

"*He's* one of those things too?" I gasped. Of course, he was. They were brothers, so why not? "How many of these dragons are there?"

"A few," Nadia said. "This town is their home. It's in another realm. Again, I know this is a lot to take in."

Another. Fucking. *Realm*? She had to be joking. "So, I'm not even on Earth anymore? I'm not in some fancy small European country? I'm in another... what? Dimension?"

Nadia winced. "Kind of. There's a magical veil we cross over to get here that separates the world we know from theirs. There are other shifters and witches and—"

"This is impossible." I shook my head and slowly got to my feet. "This is *insane*."

"But it's true!" Sarah put a hand on my arm and urged me to sit with her again. "And you know it's true because your heart just... knows that it is! We wouldn't lie to you. We didn't lie about

Lucian, either. He's special and thinks the world of you. You're..." She looked down and shook her head, as if she wanted to say more but wasn't sure if she should.

"I'm *what*, Sarah?" I pressed, using my firmest voice.

"You're his fated mate," she whispered. "That's part of why he's losing so much control whenever he's with you. The two of you are meant to be together as one."

That was the icing on the cake for me. "Fated mate? Like a *soulmate*?"

"Yes, exactly like that!" Sarah exclaimed. "He left the ceremony because he saw you for the first time and just the sight of you pulled at his inner dragon. If he hadn't left, he'd have made a huge scene in front of everyone! While the servants in the castle and his family understand, I think it would have been way more than you could have handled at that point in time."

"You think?" I didn't know how to process all this information. It sounded so surreal.

"The last time he had an emotional explosion like that, he nearly destroyed a whole wing of the castle," Nadia added. "That was when he was told I was his fated mate, then realized I wasn't."

I glared at her, all of a sudden feeling possessive of Lucian. "What do you mean he was told you were his?"

"A witch told him that one of my sisters belonged to him," Sarah said gently. "He didn't realize I had more than one, so when he met Nadia and the mating call didn't pull at him like it should have, he got upset." She gave my arm a squeeze. "And then he saw you and freaked out even more because he saw his true love did exist after all."

"True love? He barely knows me!" I certainly didn't know anything about him beyond the fact that he was tall, dreamy, amazing in bed, a little rough around the edges, and apparently, a dragon. We'd clicked right away, yes. Our chemistry was incredible. He'd certainly made love to me like he meant it.

I just struggled with the fact that he actually *did* mean it.

Guys who looked like Lucian didn't date chubby girls like me. We were fun for a little while, but not the kind of woman most guys wanted hanging on their arm in public, let alone be married to. Sure, our sparkling personalities were hard to match, but there were smart, funny, *skinny* women out there.

How could a woman who looked like me be the soulmate of a guy who might as well have been a god? I didn't believe it.

"This is ridiculous," I said, shaking my head. "You're both full of it."

"Kat!" Nadia huffed. "You're the one being ridiculous here. I get the dragon part is a stretch, but you've seen the shifting with your own eyes. You've experienced some of the magic when you crossed over the veil to get here. Haven't you noticed how different this place is from home?"

"Yes," I admitted. This place was vastly different from home. "But there is no way I'm the soulmate of Lucian! There's just no way. Whoever told him that was seriously wrong."

I stood and this time neither of my sisters stopped me. "Maybe she had it wrong and it really is you, Nadia."

"Trust me, it's not," Nadia said. "I feel absolutely nothing for him. It does go both ways. We might be human, but we also have hearts capable of discerning the truth. Don't you feel it? Deep inside of you?"

Yes. I felt it.

My heart ached for him in a whole new sort of way. I'd never felt anything like it, and that was saying quite a bit, since I had the tendency to fall for the wrong guy all the time. One look, one kind word, and hope ignited within me. Fluffy, cute hope.

Lucian did something else to me completely. I didn't merely hope for him. I *craved* him like a drug. I needed him to survive. We might have been in the beginning stages of getting to know one another, but I knew for certain the places we would be going together were amazing.

I didn't dare admit any of those thoughts to my sisters. Instead, I said nothing. They claimed to not lie to me, so I would give them that same courtesy.

"I'm going home," I somehow managed to get out. In truth, I wanted to break down into deep sobs. And then I wanted Lucian's arms wrapped around me.

God. Too many emotions had been stirred within me. Lucian was a dragon, for goodness' sake! In retrospect, he'd been a beautiful creature to behold, even in such a terrifying form. Magical and terrifying, but beautiful.

However, his lack of control scared me. So much raw passion inside of one man could easily lead to my heart snapping in two. Who was I kidding? It already had! I'd bounced from the high of a one-night stand, to the hope of starting a relationship with a guy who had fangs and claws and scales, to being told he was my *soulmate.*

My one true love.

That last one hurt the most. If they were wrong, I'd never bounce back from that level of hurt.

"Do you need help with your stuff?" Nadia asked.

"No. I want to be alone," I said, and began to walk away, then stopped at the top of the stairs. "How can I get back, anyway? You said I'm in another realm."

I couldn't believe I was actually saying that out loud, and meaning it!

Sarah let out a heavy sigh. "I'll talk to someone about giving you a ride home."

"Thanks." I paused. "Not just for that, but for not arguing with me about this decision. And for telling me everything. It's not your fault this is difficult. I won't shoot the messengers."

"Keep an open mind. That's the last thing I'll say about it." Sarah toyed with the gold ring now on her left hand. "I don't want you to shut yourself off from something amazing because you're scared. Or uncomfortable."

Uncomfortable was an understatement. I didn't want to get into all of that with her. For the time being, I'd do as she asked. Thinking about the possibilities stung, but I could leave the door open a crack. *I guess.* Only because I wanted more of that warmth from last night.

No. This is dangerous.

"Okay," I said. That was me not committing to, nor rejecting, her proposal.

I returned to the room that I'd been assigned upon my arrival —the one I'd barely spent any time in. The garment bag for my dress still lay across the bed, my duffel bag with all of my normal clothes next to it. I shut the door, changed into a pair of leggings and a t-shirt, returned my dress to its proper place, then walked back out of the room with all my stuff in tow.

"We can return that for you," Nadia offered.

I gratefully put my bag in her hands. "Thanks."

A man stepped forward. "I'm Damon, the owner of this castle, and Lucian's half-brother. I'm sorry to hear that you want to depart so soon, however, I'm happy to give you a lift back."

This was the king? He looked so normal. "Thank you. I appreciate that."

"Your sisters tell me you're aware of our secret," he continued. "You should know that the journey back is best made while on the back of a dragon. I wanted to give you a warning, so it didn't startle you too much. I understand this is all very new to you."

I looked him over. He had short, blond hair and gorgeous blue eyes. But he didn't look like a dragon either, just a normal, ordinary guy. Like Lucian had.

"Yes, this is definitely new," I said at last.

"You will need a warm jacket for traveling." He waved to a servant, who hurried forward with a long, fur-lined coat.

I slid it on even though I'd already layered up for the cold air outside.

"It gets very chilly when you're flying," Nadia added.

I glanced at her, ready to ask how she knew that, but the answer was clear. My sisters had been hiding things from me. Disappointment hit me, but with all the other emotions buffeting my system at the moment, my sisters' actions didn't affect me as badly as they would have in the past.

Damon waved for me to follow him outside and I did, my sisters close behind me. A solid lump started forming in my stomach. He walked a few feet away from the castle before transforming. The process was so smooth and elegant, quite different from the abrupt and chaotic way Lucian had done it in the bedroom. Damon stretched out his wings and neck, and while he was still imposing to behold, I didn't feel anywhere near as afraid.

Just a dragon, not a demon, my heart told me. *Lucian's the same way.*

I shook the thought away. How could a normal, human woman like me, be with a beautiful creature like that? Plus, where exactly was Lucian? For someone who claimed to be my soulmate, he sure had run away in a hurry. One would think he'd want to stay and help me make sense of it all.

The sooner I got home and tried to forget all of this, the better.

Nadia gave me a hug. "I'll come see you soon."

"Me, too," Sarah said.

"After your honeymoon," I insisted. "I'm okay, ladies. I just need to return to something familiar and then I'll be fine."

"I understand," Sarah said. "When Lucian comes back, we'll be sure to tell him."

"Sure thing." *If* he came back. I wasn't going to hold my breath, not with the way he'd been so quick to flee. We were *not* soulmates. We couldn't be. Dragons might be real, but I didn't want to be a part of their strange and unfamiliar world.

I gazed over at Damon and sucked in a deep breath, not wanting to climb on his back but desperate to return home. "I'll let you know once I'm settled in."

Damon lowered himself to the ground so I could get on his back.

For fuck's sake. I held back a half-hysterical need to laugh. My life was seriously upside down right now.

I took a step toward him and climbed up on his shiny, hard back like I would a horse, swinging my leg over then lying down flat.

Oh my God.

Once I was settled, he raised his body up and flapped his powerful wings.

I screamed, because I couldn't help it.

"Hold on!" Sarah called out.

She didn't have to tell me twice! I grabbed onto what bit of him I could and clung for dear life. As we rose in the air, I closed my eyes tightly. However high up we were going, I didn't need to see it, right? I just had to trust he would get me over—or was it through?—the magic veil in one piece.

We soared through the atmosphere, and there was a strange tingling against my skin. For a second, I opened my eyes and saw a shimmer in the sky—a shift in the very fabric of existence—but before I could focus on it properly, we had passed through. That must have been the veil. Immediately, I noticed a difference in the air.

It was normal again. Warmer, too.

Damon glided through the air for a few more miles before finding a place to land. Once I slid off his back, I stroked his scales in thanks, still weirded out by the dragon body, but not terrified anymore. A step in the right direction. My brother-in-law was a dragon. I didn't have to be part of their world, but I did need to accept it if I had any hope of maintaining a relationship with Sarah.

He shifted back to human for a moment, and I averted my eyes to avoid staring at his nakedness. If I was honest, he did nothing for me. Not like Lucian.

"From here, will you be able to make your way home?" he asked.

"Yes, thank you," I said. "It's not far."

"I'm going to take a moment to rest and make sure you get a ride back. Then I'll be on my way."

Such a gentleman. Lucian had been as well. Had I been too quick to judge him? Maybe. But he'd still left me and stayed away. That was the other thing—he hadn't come back. He'd barely tried, and that spoke volumes to me.

I used my phone to call for a ride, glad I had that and my purse on me. It didn't take long for a car to get there. By the time I got back to my house, I was absolutely exhausted.

Exhausted and heartbroken. I'd taken a leap of faith last night by letting Lucian charm me into his bed. Once again, it was a misplaced hope.

Our two worlds did not belong together.

Lucian

I stayed at the small house in the woods for two days. During that time, I did everything in my power to regain control over my emotions. I talked myself into returning to the castle to properly woo my mate, only to talk myself out of it again.

Since I was already there, I tried to sort through the lingering baggage from my father. Perhaps I should have turned around and returned within a few hours, but I felt like I owed it to Katerina to sort through the toxic emotions brewing inside me.

If I didn't, how could I ever love her the way she deserved to be loved?

I was proud of myself for coming back at all. Those dark places in my heart still tried to tell me I should stay away; that I wasn't worthy.

Katerina should have cooled off a while ago, and her sisters must have told her everything about our world by now. Once she knew we were fated mates, she'd welcome me back with open arms. Or that was my hope, anyway.

I landed within the castle grounds, slightly unnerved by how quiet it was. The wedding festivities were obviously well over. Most of the mess had been cleaned up. I walked into the palace, looking for evidence of my mate.

"Katerina?" I called out. My voice echoed through the halls. "Katerina, where are you?"

A soft clearing of the throat startled me. One of the servants was hiding by the doorframe. "She's... returned to the human realm."

"What?" My hands clenched into fists, and I stormed up the stairs. "That's not possible! How did she get back there? She isn't scheduled to leave for another week, at least."

Hadn't that been the original plan? Sarah's out-of-town family were to stay for a while.

"It's true, sir. We cleaned up her room today," the servant said from below.

I stalked to the room that had belonged to Katerina and found it empty and far too pristine. Sadness crushed the hope in my chest. "Why did you leave?" I spoke to the empty walls. "I don't understand."

The memory of her calling me a demon crept back into my head. Had she left, because she truly believed I was evil?

She was supposed to stay so we could talk. Why didn't anyone try to stop her? Everyone knew she was my fated mate, and they all understood how important that was. I'd never have stood back and watched Sarah walk away from Dymitri.

Is it because they know I'm not good enough for her? That I'm too broken to be a worthy husband?

Were they saving both of us the heartache of disappointment? Could they see how our relationship was destined to crash and burn?

I didn't even get to say a proper goodbye. Fuck! I'd screwed up royally. If only I'd managed to control myself, then none of this would have happened. We could have languished in our bliss for a while longer, and then I would have gently brought her into my world, the way I'd planned to, originally. But, no, I had to act like an animal. No wonder she'd left. If the situation was reversed, I wouldn't stay, either.

I sighed and walked toward my room. Anger and hurt still pulsed through me, and I needed to be alone to squash it down before I destroyed even more of the castle. Why did I have to be such an idiot?

Somehow, I had to work out how to become resigned to a life of solitude. I accepted Katerina's rejection with a heavy heart, and tried to think of ways to fill my time.

I could at least make things right for my brothers, by fixing all the damage I'd caused to the castle. They'd suffered considerably because of my lack of self-control. Then once I was done, I'd see to it that I never caused harm again.

My initial instincts had been right. I knew too little about love to be able to give it to another. Fated mate or not, if I couldn't behave the way a man should, I'd never succeed.

I didn't try to find Nadia or Sarah. I just changed into warmer clothes and began repairs on the damage I'd caused, starting with the stonework. Using my body in a physical way kept me distracted from my feelings, at least a little. Laying brick and mortar down gave me a different kind of satisfaction. With each slab I placed came a piece of healing to my soul. I might not forgive myself, but I could earn forgiveness from my brothers. They'd said it was all water under the bridge, but I didn't believe them. I could feel the burden I'd placed on them unnecessarily.

A week passed, then two, filled with long days of work. My progress on the castle repairs was steady and when I wasn't fixing what I'd broken, I dove headfirst into training.

I'd always kept myself physically active, but the need to exhaust myself so I couldn't think about *her* was great, indeed. If I could lay my head on the pillow at the end of the day and fall straight to sleep from pure exhaustion, that was a good day. Unfortunately, by that definition, most of my days were bad. No matter how hard I pushed myself, I always had a few thoughts left for Katerina. Memories of her smile, her body, her warmth. My inner dragon yearned for her. *I* yearned for her... the sweet taste of love I didn't deserve.

After too many nights without sleep, tortured by my memories, I began to push myself twice as hard.

My brothers checked in on me from time to time. They weren't wrong to do so, since I was battling depression like I never had before. I did a fairly good job of hiding it. Or so I thought.

"Still sulking?" Dymitri asked one morning.

I glanced up at him and narrowed my eyes. He was leaning against the doorframe and shook his head when I scowled. "Damon and I have a bet going on how long this pity party will continue. He seems to think you'll bounce back any day now. I, on the other hand, know you're stubborn enough to continue in this vein forever."

I snorted. "It's nice to know my misery is amusing to you both."

"It's far from amusing, actually," he said, and walked toward me. "I want to lose this wager, so prove me wrong, brother. Snap out of this funk and return to the human realm so you can win Katerina back."

"She left me!" I snapped. "And she had every reason to. I lost myself in my dragon. I frightened her, just like I did with Nadia. I fucked up, just like I always do. She deserves someone mature. When women say they want a man who would kill for them, they never mean it literally."

"True." Dymitri nodded, considering my words. "That being said, I don't think you give yourself enough credit."

I shrugged. My brother was biased. He was the only person in this world who truly loved me. "She still left."

"*You* rushed off and never came back. Maybe that had something to do with her leaving?"

I glared at him. "She was about to hyperventilate! She thought I was going to *eat* her! What was I supposed to do? Let her pass out?"

"You stay and you calm her down!" He pinched the bridge of his nose. "Running away is the perfect way to make a woman to feel unwanted."

"Right. I fucked up," I growled. "And that's why I'm staying away, because I don't know what I'm doing. I don't know how to love her and I'm going to keep hurting her. I'm just like Father."

"No!" He grabbed me by the shoulders and shook me hard. "You are not! You are kind and caring. Father would have laughed and tormented her. You left because you were worried for her and stayed away because you're afraid of hurting her more. Believe me, brother, I understand those feelings all too well. But every morning, I dedicate myself to proving I can be different. I think you want to do that, too. You came back. Maybe not when you should have, but you did. You returned."

I swallowed, looking away, unable to take the weight of his gaze any longer. "I didn't mean to wait so long. I couldn't return until I was at peace with myself. Then I got here and unraveled all over again."

"You didn't decimate the building this time," Dymitri pointed out with a smirk. "You're making progress."

I let out a sour laugh. "There's no way I can win her back. She was so frightened. I know it's a lot to take in, but..."

"Damon flew her back, you know."

Damon? My heart lurched at the thought of my mate on the king's back. It should have been me, carrying her in that way.

"She might have been afraid, but she accepted him in dragon

form, and she will accept you too if you give her the chance." He exhaled heavily. "Lucian, there is so much happiness to be had by embracing the mate bond fully. Stop talking yourself out of the possibility. You do know that you deserve that, right? To be happy. We are not our father. We do not have to pay for his sins. Don't you miss her?"

"With every breath," I whispered.

"Why keep fighting, then?" He let out an angry huff. "Please, go to her! Talk to her! She'll understand so much more than you think."

"It's been too long."

"You're fated to be together. It doesn't matter how long it's been. Don't quit before you've even started." He closed his eyes and our foreheads touched. "It'll be okay."

Hopefully he was right. I closed my eyes as well and took in a slow breath. "Promise?"

"I swear it." He patted my shoulder and pulled away. "I'm sure her sisters will help too."

I'd struggled with facing them. Every so often I would see Sarah in the distance and when she looked at me, all I saw was pity. So embarrassing... Nadia avoided me equally as much as I avoided her. Given our history, the last thing I needed was to hear her opinion of my latest blunder.

Naturally, Dymitri led me to Nadia rather than his wife. Of course, he did. It was as if he knew how little I wanted to see her. I let out a groan.

"Stop that," he hissed, then turned to Nadia. "You'll be nice, won't you?"

She nodded. "I won't say anything bad. Promise." She stared up at me. "I'm sure you already know how the conversation would go. Imagine your worst, and just pretend it was all actually said. How's that?"

My jaw tightened. "That isn't nice, Nadia."

I instantly regretted my words. Her eyes flashed, and even though she held her tongue, I understood right away just how much she was holding back.

"I'm sorry," I mumbled. "And yes, I have imagined our conversation and it was pretty rough."

Her mouth lifted in a little smile. "I bet it was."

"Can you help me get to Katerina?"

"Of course." She smiled properly then, tears pooling in her eyes. "I want you two to have all the happiness in the world."

I let out a sigh of relief. "Be honest, then, please. Do you think it's too late?"

"No. But we shouldn't make her wait any longer, right?" She winked, then frowned. "Wait, you're not going to wear *that*, are you?"

I looked down at my clothes to see what was wrong with them. I'd been wearing old, ripped jeans and a gray sweatshirt because they were easier to work in. The fact that they were currently covered in dust probably made them not the best choice of clothing, I had to admit.

"An outfit change isn't necessary," Dymitri said. "He'll be shifting anyway."

That was true. I'd end up naked on the other side of the veil if I wasn't organized.

"Fine," Nadia said. "I suppose you're right. She'll just be happy he's at her door."

Hope ignited within me. "Do you think so?"

"I know so. Come on."

She grabbed a large cloak from the front door hook, and we hurried out of the castle. I was so eager to get going I just about took off without Nadia, but then I remembered I couldn't find Katerina without her sister's help. I needed an address, and someone to make sure I didn't change my mind and turn around.

"Want me to carry your clothes?" she asked, rather sensibly.

"Yes. Thank you." I stripped off and folded the clothes, handing her the jeans and shirt before letting go of my humanity and shifting into my dragon.

The small seeds of doubt planted so deeply by my father had grown for a long time and they still threatened to rear up.

Dymitri is right, though. I am not my father, nor should I be punished for his sins. Just because Father never loved me, doesn't mean a thing. All it proves is how terrible a person he actually was.

Nadia climbed onto my back, and we flew into the sky. I took her across the veil and into the human realm, praying the whole way that she was right and that I hadn't left it too late to fix things with Katerina.

Katerina

"Miss Kat! Miss Kat!" One of my students ran over holding up her latest drawing of... a bear? *I think that's what it's supposed to be.* "I made this for you!"

"It's beautiful," I said, taking the drawing and setting it on my desk. "I especially love your use of purple and blue. Did you know those were my two favorite colors?"

The little girl nodded enthusiastically. "I hope you feel happier soon!"

"I'm very happy," I said, meaning it in that moment.

All my kindergarteners made life a million times better for me. I loved them so much. Even when they acted out and frustrated me to tears, I wouldn't have traded them for any other job. There was always *something* to smile about.

"Okay," the girl said and shrugged, almost like she didn't believe me.

Kids had a way of being able to read me better than most adults. They were also far more honest and braver than anyone gave them credit for. I'd never tell her just how much happier her noticing my sadness made me feel.

I looked at the clock. "All right, class, it's time to start cleaning up so we can get ready to go home!"

The kids all excitedly tidied up their tables. I couldn't help but share their excitement. So much so, that I opted to bring all my work back home with me to do there rather than stay at school for my usual extra two hours after class had been dismissed.

I loved my job but was exhausted at the moment. Ever since my adventure across the veil, I hadn't felt like myself. My body just wasn't as energetic as it used to be, and I'd wondered—several times—if maybe the magic messed me up somehow. Was that possible? I was an ordinary human, after all. I didn't belong over there. What if my molecules had scrambled when I crossed over? Was that why I felt like death warmed over every morning? Like I could never get enough sleep.

The exhaustion was more than physical. It was mental, too. My mind kept wandering back to the night of the wedding, the night I'd spent with Lucian. Not just the incredible sex we'd had, but all the subtler ways he'd expressed his desire for me. The intense gaze across the room, the hands catching me as I almost fell, the smile... oh, the smile. All those memories haunted me like a ghost with unfinished business.

Then I'd remember the huge dragon, and how scared I'd been when he first shifted. And the fact that he'd left me and hadn't so much as *tried* to contact me since then. It had been more than two weeks. If we were supposed to be together, then where was he?

The whole experience was an emotional rollercoaster and it was just too much to deal with.

I drove home early from the school, glad it was Friday and the weekend was around the corner. I'd have a couple of days to regroup and eat a pint of ice cream... or three. Maybe. That was how I normally comforted myself after a difficult week, yet even the thought of my beloved Chocolate Chip Cookie Dough left me feeling nauseous. How sad was that?

In short, I was a hot mess, and the stress was taking its toll. Even my period was late in protest. That only freaked me out a little. Okay, more than a little, but I was determined to not jump to conclusions until more time had passed. Periods could be late for all kinds of reasons, not just because I'd had unprotected sex with a dragon.

I shook the idea out of my head. Nope, not going to doom-spiral over a "what if".

And I hated that I'd let myself get so emotionally crazed over a one-night stand. I went into his room with the intention of just enjoying myself. One night of hot passion and then letting him go, because he'd *want* to be set free. With that expectation, I shouldn't have ended up getting hurt.

He just had to be a freaking dragon, didn't he?

Fated soulmate business aside, just the fact that he was a shifter blew my mind several times over. I'd grown up not believing in much beyond what I could observe.

If I could see it, taste it, touch it and so on, then I knew it was real and true. It would make sense. People shifting into dragons? *Actual* dragons? That was harder to pull into my sphere of logic. Magic was for fairytales, and fairytales weren't real.

Well, I'd had that belief blown right out of the water, that's for sure.

I'd seen it with my own eyes. I'd heard his roar. Felt the scales on Damon's back as he carried me back here to my own world. My five senses were backing up the truth—dragons *were* real.

I walked into my house and did the first thing I did every day when I got home from work—checked in on my sick father. Part of the reason I lived away from Nadia and Sarah was so that I could take care of him. As the oldest, that duty fell on my shoulders. Okay, it was also something I chose. My sisters did not need to help shoulder the burden. I handled it fine on my own.

How are you feeling today? I texted. He usually was awake at this time.

Feeling good! Which didn't mean much, but we celebrated all those small victories.

Love you! I'll be in to visit soon. I promised.

I set the phone down, knowing he probably wanted to talk more but I just couldn't do it. My head and heart weren't in the right space for a full conversation. If I started talking to him, he'd know something was wrong. That's why I texted instead of called. He couldn't hear the waver in my voice through a text message.

Looking forward to it. Love you too.

I stared at those words, feeling guilty. My dad meant the world to me. He'd helped hold me together more times than I could count. I almost changed my mind and called him so we could talk about all my life problems. Almost.

Telling him I'd had an intense night of sexual relations with the hottest man alive was probably going to be too much information. Telling him that man was also a dragon, might have him questioning my sanity. Pretending everything was okay would result in me spilling my guts. No, I had to wait. We'd catch up later.

I sighed, at a loss for what to do.

If Nadia and Sarah were home, then maybe I'd call them. Sarah was staying in the other realm, apparently. Nadia wasn't planning on coming back just yet, so I'd have to wait to talk to her, too. We hadn't always been super-close, but there was comfort in knowing they were around. Having them not be a phone call away left a strange void in my life.

They were a part of Lucian's world now. That magical place with the dragons. Sarah had married one, and Nadia sure seemed attached to castle life despite not having a dragon of her own. And just like that, my mind was back on Lucian and the night we'd spent together.

Lucian was *my* dragon. I had one to love and call my own.

Had, being the keyword there. Past tense. He might have felt drawn to me initially, but that clearly didn't last.

I rummaged through my refrigerator, knowing I should eat something but not really wanting to. Partly because of the exhaustion and nausea constantly lurking under the surface, and partly because maybe if I was a little more mindful of what I ate, then I could be more attractive. Because I'd be, well, *smaller*.

Stupid train of thought, I know. But I kept going back to one fact—I wasn't a size two. I wasn't even a size six. I was a size sixteen. Full-on curves and rolls. I'd always looked this way. Whatever cute, petite genetics my sisters had gotten from our parents completely bypassed me.

Most days, I accepted it. Embraced it, even. When I looked in the mirror, I saw beauty staring back at me. I'd had enough long-term boyfriends to know that I was loveable. But all those boyfriends had eventually moved onto a smaller version of me. Seeing them with their new girlfriends always brought on the doubt. Had I been lied to? And lied to myself? Was I really not worthy of being loved, after all?

And that's where my head went every time I thought of Lucian. We'd had an amazing time together. I let myself give in to his charms because I'd instantly felt safe *and* desirable. I didn't just feel beautiful when I looked into his eyes, I felt out-of-this-world gorgeous. Like he only had eyes for me, and no one could ever turn his head elsewhere. For once, someone saw my true worth.

It was that thought that made me miss him more than I should. Our instant, magnetic attraction to one another that continued to attempt to cloud my logic. I'd gone in with no expectations for more, and left thinking there would be far more than I ever imagined possible. Even post-dragon grand reveal and return to my human reality, I'd spent a few days hoping he'd knock on my front door.

Soulmate. I'm not sure how much of that I bought, anyway. It always felt like a line any time I'd heard it.

"You wouldn't understand. She's my soulmate. You aren't." That's how it usually went.

But why did I let myself get so caught up in him? Why was I still letting myself get lost in those dark eyes? Why couldn't I just let him go? Why did I feel like my heart was being ripped in half for a man I barely knew?

None of it made sense.

I groaned, settling down with the small serving of leftover pasta I'd discovered in the fridge. I didn't put anything on it. Bland sounded soothing to my upset stomach. Once again, just thinking of Lucian had my belly in knots.

I'd taken two bites when there was a knock on my door.

I scowled toward the sound. Who would be coming to my house?

I peeked through the peephole and my mouth dropped open. Was I seeing right? I swung the door open and stood there gaping. Nadia was standing on my front stoop.

With Lucian beside her.

SEVEN

Lucian

Nadia motioned for me to knock on the door. "Go on. You can do it."

"I can," I whispered, my breath short with nervous tension. I raised my hand and knocked against the wooden surface, waiting, hoping, praying that Katerina didn't slam the door in my face the moment she saw me.

The door opened wide, and Katerina stood in front of us, her eyes widening as she gazed briefly at her sister then up at me. "You... you came?"

"Yes," I said, my heart beating hard and fast.

Damn, she's beautiful.

She stood there, staring at me almost as if she expected something more. After a moment, her gaze shifted back to her sister, and she frowned. "O... kay?"

Nadia nudged me.

"May I come in so we can talk?" I asked, my heart pounding even louder in my ears with every passing second. I could barely focus. The moment Katerina appeared, my body craved hers, and my heart sang in a way I'd never thought possible.

I'd never experienced such a reaction before.

"I don't know," Katerina said. "I'm not sure I have anything to say to you."

"Please," I stressed.

"You had your chance to talk to me before," she pointed out. "And you didn't take it."

"It's hard to get a word in when you're screaming your head off," I grumbled. Nadia gave me a sharp elbow in the side. "Ow."

She glared up at me, and didn't need to say more.

Control my temper. Message received.

I took a slow breath and released it in a measured way. "I would very much like to talk to you. May I please come in so I can do so?"

For a few seconds, Katerina didn't say anything. I wasn't sure if she'd heard me.

Eventually, she stepped aside. "Uh, yeah... I guess."

Not the elated reaction I'd been hoping to receive. I almost turned and left. Being an asshole for self-preservation reasons was better than sitting in her living room so she could reject me all over again. I'd promised myself I'd do right by her, though, and I was determined to stick with it.

Nadia pushed me through the door as if she could sense my urge to flee.

I staggered inside and sat down on a chair in her living room.

"Sure, make yourself comfortable," Katerina mumbled. "No problem."

I scowled. What was I doing wrong *now*?

Before I could say anything, Nadia spoke up. "Since you two are getting settled so nicely, I'm going to head out. Kat, call me later, okay?"

"Okay," Katerina said softly. I could tell she didn't want her sister to leave us alone.

Nadia hurried away and the front door closed with a resounding thud. A long silence passed between Katerina and me.

"How have you been?" I asked, wanting to fill the silence.

"Confused," she said. She stared down at me from where she stood. Why wouldn't she sit? Her arms were folded across her chest in a less than inviting stance. "It's a lot, you know. Having you turn into a... a..."

"Dragon?" I supplied.

She nodded. "Yeah, that. It would have been nice to receive a gentle introduction to the idea."

"I agree. That's what I had planned to give you. It's why I tried to leave before you could see me change." I gazed down at my hands and sighed. "For that, I apologize. I should have had better control. I was too excited. After so long wondering if I had—no, *hoping* I had—a fated mate, I discovered it was true. At long last, you were there. The one thing I'd dreamed of—the other half of my soul. My fated mate."

"See, that's the part I think is shit," she said. "There's no way *I'm* the girl you'd been dreaming about. I couldn't be."

Why did she always doubt me? "I'm not lying."

"Explain it to me better, please. All of it. Nothing about this makes any sense."

"Sit," I said. "Please. I think it'll be easier to listen."

She huffed and rolled her eyes but did what I said. "Fine."

Without her looming over me, I felt more confident. Where to begin, though? "You've seen that I can turn into a dragon. I think that part doesn't need to be talked about in any more detail."

"Well, maybe, but I do actually have questions about that, too," she said. "There's a lot about it I don't understand. How? Why? And where were we exactly, for that matter? How different is your home from here? Were you born like that? Was everybody in your... realm... able to change into a dragon, too?"

Her questions helped guide me with what to answer first. "The how and why are the same, I suppose. I'm a shifter. It's what we do. We can change into the creature of our bloodline. In my case, that's a dragon. There are others. Bears, wolves, just about any animal, to be honest. There are some humans and non-shifters who live among us, too. But those of us who can shift... yes, we are born that way. We live with both human instincts and those of our animal form. Dragons are by far the most regal and sentient of the bunch, in my opinion."

"I can see that," she said. "And the why you change is just... because that's what you do?"

"Yes. It's just what we do." I ran my hands over my jeans, my nerves slowly starting to fade. Her decreasing hostility gave me hope. "As for where... we were staying in my brother's castle on the other side of the veil. Over there, my kind are normal."

I gazed at her as I spoke. Our eyes met, and my heart fluttered in my chest. "Over in my realm, our territories are divided by kingdoms, much like the world you live in. Unlike your world, though, there are still kings to rule them. My brother, Damon, is one of those kings."

She blinked. "So, you're a prince?"

"No." I said. "We're half-brothers. Same father, different mothers. My mother, who I share with Dymitri, was not the queen. When my father passed on, Damon took over to rule the kingdom. However, I don't have any birthright to the throne. Damon is gracious and has said Dymitri and I are welcome on his lands. A stark change from my father's attitude toward us."

"Your dad didn't want you around?" She gasped. "Are you serious?"

"Yes." I shifted in my chair, not caring to dwell on this part of my story. It was the part that had kept me away from her, after all.

I cleared my throat before she could say more. "Anyway, I have slowly learned to accept my brother Damon's hospitality. Actually, I'm still learning, I think. We are dragons of the north. He seems to think all of us should work as a unit to unite the kingdom. My father wasn't the best of rulers, as I'm sure you can imagine."

Katerina nodded slowly. "My sisters mentioned something about soul mates?"

"Fated mates," I clarified. "We call them fated mates. Every shifter is born with one. You are the other half of my soul. When we are together, we feel whole because our souls are bonded as one at last."

"If that's the case, why did Nadia say you thought she was your fated mate?" Her gaze narrowed. "I know you said a witch told you, but that feels awfully convenient for an out. How do I know you're not just using that as an excuse?"

I wanted to know who had hurt her so badly to make her distrust me so deeply. "Marienne can see things others can't because of her magic. She is a sorceress and if you would like to meet her, we could organize a trip to her castle. But her magic isn't completely reliable. What she told me was that my fated mate was Sarah's sister. I didn't know about you, and I made the mistake of assuming it was Nadia. However, the moment I laid eyes on your younger sister, I knew she wasn't the one. Everyone else told me to give it time and the instinct would kick in once she awakened from her injuries. It never did. My gut was right. She wasn't the one. I didn't even try to pursue her."

I had to make that last part clear.

"So, you just... knew? The moment you saw her?" Katerina asked. "And when you saw me, you knew I *was* the one? How does that work?"

"The dragon inside of me recognized the other half of my soul instantly," I explained. "That's how I knew Nadia wasn't the one despite everyone's insistence. Initially, I thought Marienne's magic had been wrong. That there was no hope for me. Part of me thought…" I swallowed, unsure if I wanted to confess the truth. But to gain more of Katerina's trust, I had to show her all of me. "Part of me thought that perhaps I didn't have a fated mate at all. That I was impossible to love."

Katerina's frown deepened. "Why would your mind ever go there?"

"Remember, I'd been cast out by my father."

"So?"

"So, if he couldn't love me, how could I expect anyone else to do so?" It made sense in my head.

Katerina shook her head. "Right. Your dad who *chose* to not love you. That is different than *couldn't*. And I don't know a whole lot about the situation, but of the few things you've just said, I don't know why you'd let this one guy dictate your self-worth. He's clearly an asshole."

"Yes, yes he was." I chuckled. Rather than try to explain in another way, I let the topic drop for the time being. "Regardless of how logical my reasoning is or isn't, I'd come to terms with the idea of being alone. Then you entered the castle and all of that changed. I wanted to properly woo you. To bring you into my world and show you the possibilities of our future together. And then I messed it all up."

"Turning into a dragon first thing in the morning is definitely far from a gentle introduction," Katerina said.

A small smile lifted her lips as she spoke. My heart jumped. I was making ground.

"I left because I didn't want you to go into shock. While I was gone, I came up with all the reasons I should stay away." I held up a hand when she opened her mouth, probably to protest. "I know it's no excuse. Leaving, and especially not returning, was not the right course of action to take. In the moment, I wanted to protect you. Then, I decided you could do so much better than me."

She laughed. "Funny, I've been thinking the same thing myself. That you could do better than *me*."

That broke my heart to hear. "But you're perfection."

She gazed at me for a second, then cleared her throat. "What now?"

"I want another chance. I want to show you how true our connection is." I gazed down at my hands in my lap. "Please, Katerina, will you forgive me for running off?"

"I can't deny there is a connection," she said softly. "I felt it that night, and I feel it now. As much as I tell myself there's nothing going on, nothing between us, I know it's a lie. Fighting it is starting to get exhausting."

"Then we can return to my realm and—"

She shook her head. "No, I'm not going back there. It's cold and bleak and my life is here! I have a class of students who are counting on me, as well as my dad. If Sarah and Nadia stay over there, then who is going to look after him? He's really sick. I'm not sure if Sarah told you. Our relationship with him isn't stellar, but I could never abandon him."

I nodded, my heart sinking once more. Rejected again. "I understand. Then I will take my leave."

"You're going?" She gasped. "Just like that?"

"If you don't want me..."

"I said I'm not going back to your realm," she snapped. "But you can stay here... with me. If you want to."

My heart began to beat faster at the idea, excitement and fear pulsing through me. She wanted me to stay! However, staying in the human realm would be tricky. No other shifters. I'd be forced to live the life of a human man. Was I capable of *only* being human? What if I couldn't blend in?

But when I looked at Katerina, with her big, beautiful eyes and stunning face, I couldn't refuse. This was my chance to prove to her that I wanted her. All of her.

I nodded. "All right, I'll stay with you. Long enough for us to figure out something more long-term."

"Sure," she mumbled. "I'll get some blankets and pillows for you so you're comfortable on the couch."

"The... couch." I looked down at the far-too-small-for-my-large-frame piece of furniture and swallowed uncomfortably. A loud and clear message if there ever was one. She didn't want to share her bed with me.

She disappeared down a nearby hallway, then I heard a door open and close again. "You got lucky once. I'm not ready to be so... intimate with you. I have a lot to think about, and a lot has changed."

"For the better, I hope."

When she returned, she held a small pile of blankets and pillows. She was smiling, so I took that as a good sign. "I'm looking forward to getting to know you better. Right now, that's all I can promise. You wanted a chance."

"Yes." More than anything.

"This is it." She handed me the blankets. "Now, I was just eating dinner. Are you hungry?"

I nodded. My stomach still churned with nerves, but I would do anything for my one true mate. Every second we had to bond, I was going to take, even if it meant living in a foreign world. And sleeping on a tiny couch.

We ate, and Katerina told me more about her world. The small details about her life and more about the people she loved. Her students and how happy they made her.

Then we watched a television show she liked, and I sat through the whole thing despite not understanding the storyline.

She told me about the music she enjoyed listening to when she needed to relax. I took mental notes about everything.

Finally, she yawned. The clock on the wall read midnight.

"I should get some sleep," she said. "Can't believe we stayed up this late."

I could, and I didn't want the night to end.

"Sleep well," I forced myself to say even though watching her leave me was the last thing I wanted.

But she smiled and turned away and I watched her go. My dragon rumbled inside me but didn't fight hard against me. He knew we needed to take our time with her as well. She needed to be seduced, so we would just have to be patient.

I stood up, my body aching for my mate. *Fuck*. I ran my hands through my hair, a loud groan filling my throat. Get a grip and get ready for bed.

I arranged the pillows and the blankets, stripped out of my dusty clothes and climbed on to my makeshift bed, folding up my legs to try and fit. I wouldn't get much sleep on the tiny thing, but at least I could rest a little, knowing I was in my mate's house.

We might have been separated in body, but in spirit, I felt a whole lot closer.

EIGHT

Katerina

Lucian and I spent the whole weekend in my house, just talking and getting to know each other better. I studied his mannerisms and tried to decipher all the words he wasn't saying. He seemed like a genuine guy and I could sense he was actually telling the truth when he spoke.

But doubt crept in anyway, although that might have had something to do with the fact that my period was still late. Now it was late by five days—almost a full week—and I couldn't blame it on stress any longer.

"I'm going to the grocery store," I announced Sunday evening.

"We've already eaten," Lucian said, as though that was the only reason to go shopping.

"I'm out of coffee," I managed. It wasn't a lie, so I didn't feel guilty using that as an excuse. If my suspicions were right though, I wouldn't be drinking coffee for a while.

I went to the nearest store and got myself a pregnancy test. Completely distracted, I'd already paid for it when I realized I was about to go home with no coffee, so I doubled back and grabbed a bag of my favorite roasted beans.

Being away from Lucian felt... wrong. I missed him even for the few minutes I was in the store. Or rather, I missed the way I felt around him.

I thought about telling him what I was doing, I truly did. Having him with me as I bought the test then took it, would have stopped my body from shaking so much with stress.

But until I knew for sure what the result was, I didn't want to say anything. Why ruin the beginning of a possible new relationship with unnecessary drama?

When I got home, I put the test in the bathroom so I could take it after he fell asleep. But the joke was on me, and I fell asleep on the couch, my head on his lap, while we watched a movie. Eventually, I did make it back to my room, but I was too tired to worry about the test.

First thing in the morning, I couldn't put it off any longer. My alarm clock went off at five a.m., and I'd run out of excuses. Lucian was still sleeping on the couch, so I had the privacy I needed.

As my stomach flipped with anxiety, I summoned the courage to creep to the bathroom and find the box I'd stashed there. I took the test and did my makeup while waiting for the results. That was the only thing I could think of to distract myself so I didn't pace in front of the clock and accidentally wake Lucian. My hands shook the whole time, so it was a miracle I didn't end up looking like a clown.

Five minutes passed slowly. I checked the test. Positive.

My heart fell. "No," I whispered. "No, no, no."

I blinked back hot tears as I disposed of the evidence in the trash beneath used tissues and other random items. I didn't want Lucian to see the test before I could talk to him... and that wouldn't be happening until after I got home from work.

Hopefully that would give me enough time to figure out what

to say—and what I was going to do. No, I couldn't make a decision without discussing the situation with him. That wouldn't be fair. But I should at least think about it first.

He's going to be so pissed.

Thoughts of impending doom raced through my mind while I waited for my coffee to brew. A coffee I couldn't drink because of the caffeine but made out of habit all the same.

It sat in my thermal mug all day, mocking me.

For the sake of my students and my ability to teach that day, I pushed any worry about Lucian's reaction out of my brain. The thoughts kept trying to creep in, and I squashed them down until three o'clock.

As soon as my kiddos were on the bus, I closed the door to the classroom, sat down at my desk and cried. Full-on ugly sobbing.

I just got Lucian back and now he's going to leave again.

According to him, finding out I was his true mate had sent him spiraling out of control. A baby was going to push him over the edge. Talk about a life-altering change! We were going to be responsible for raising another human being.

Or were we?

Horror filled my chest, making the tears dry up. What if the baby came out a dragon? What if it came out with scales and magic? Was I even going to be able to give birth to it?

I'd seen the long talons and sharp teeth on Lucian when he was in dragon from. No way was I going to be able to push out a creature like that from my body without suffering some sort of damage. I probably wouldn't even survive!

Just the thought of giving birth to a normal baby terrified me. I'd heard it was the most painful experience a woman could go through. But a *dragon*?

And I'm going to get bigger. Even bigger than I already am.

There was no way I could avoid that. The baby would be growing inside of me, and I in turn, would get even fatter. I tried to imagine myself pregnant and didn't like what I saw in my imagination. Would people even realize I *was* pregnant? Or would they assume the worst about me?

I knew for a fact I wouldn't be one of those cute girls who looked like they'd shoved a basketball up her t-shirt. I'd look like a hippo.

If Lucian and I had been together for longer than a handful of hours, I might have felt less insecure. Even better—if the baby had been planned and not the result of a one-night stand. But circumstances weren't ideal, so my brain was on overdrive and my self-esteem was at a record low.

He was never going to stay with me, and he certainly wouldn't look at me with desire once I turned into a pumpkin.

"This can't be happening," I whispered.

I looked up at the clock and knew I had to get back home. Lucian was waiting and somehow, I had to find the words to tell him my news.

I drove home and rehearsed a number of approaches. Funny, cute, serious, matter of fact.

Hey, guess what? You knocked me up with one try. Pretty good, huh?

There were too many options, and I didn't know him well enough to guess which would work best.

He's a no-nonsense kind of guy, I think. So maybe I'll just state it point-blank.

When I walked into my house and saw him cooking dinner, I lost all my nerve. *I'm only a few weeks along. Maybe the test is a false positive.*

Yes, that made perfect sense.

Besides, what if something happens and I lose it?

That thought scared me just as much as having a baby did. I couldn't lose it. I didn't want to. But I wasn't far along, and a lot could change in a week. Look what had happened in just the last few hours.

And there he was, standing in my kitchen cooking dinner for me. His large form, performing such an ordinary domestic chore, gave me butterflies in the belly. Even the smile he shot in my direction as I walked in the door was perfection. Why destroy that the beginning of something that could be beautiful, when everything was still so new and fragile?

I'll wait a week or two. That'll give me more time to prepare, and us more time to know if what we have is real.

And more importantly, if it was going to last.

"You're home later than I thought," he said. "Though, that's for the better, because dinner might be a little delayed."

I set my purse down. "What brought this on?"

"What?" he asked.

"You cooking dinner," I said, gesturing to the stove. I leaned against the wall near the kitchen counter. "You're a guest, remember?"

He was so beautiful. Way too good for me.

"I thought the best way to get on your good side would be to make you food." He grinned.

I scowled at him, hating the inference. "Why? Because I'm fat?"

"What?" He frowned.

"The best way to get on my good side is food because I'm fat," I repeated, crossing my arms over my chest. "Fat girls love food, right? We don't like flowers or books or poems. Just lavish dinners and decadent chocolate."

He raised a brow. "Actually, the hope was to prove that I'm self-sufficient and reliable," he said coolly.

I rolled my eyes, wanting to contain my sudden annoyance but somehow unable to stop. "If you want to impress me, do the dishes when you're done and all my laundry. Then keep doing it for a week, then two, then a month, and for a whole year. Cooking one dinner doesn't prove anything to me."

"Right." He turned back to the pot on the stove and stirred vigorously. "But this dinner is a start. I thought."

It was. I couldn't argue with that, but somehow, I did anyway. What had gotten into me? "Sure, Lucian. Whatever you say."

"Why are you being so nasty?" he snapped.

I was. I couldn't deny it, and I didn't even know why. I shrugged. "I'm being realistic," I grumbled and marched off to go sit on my living room couch.

It was easy for him to say all of these things *now*. Life was still easy. We were in the honeymoon period of dating. The beginning, where everything felt magical and perfect. A place he was in, and I couldn't be, not when I had to plan ahead just in case.

And if I lost him for good, I didn't know how I would cope.

Katerina

Lucian turned down the pot on the stove and followed me to the couch. He sat next to me, his gaze never leaving my face. "Elaborate, please. I'm missing something. How is giving me sass and sarcasm being realistic?"

"It's self-preservation!" I exploded. "You can say until the cows come home that you're going to stick around and be a perfect partner for me. I'm not going to believe any of it until I see it. Sure, one dinner is a start. I get that, but you're going to ditch me. It's only a matter of time."

"Why do you doubt me?"

"Because every other guy I've been with has left!"

"I'm not them!" he seethed, his eyes flashing with anger.

I snorted. "Because you're my soulmate?"

"Yes!"

"Soulmate or not, you'll get tired of me eventually. Once you realize you can have a hotter girl..." I shook my head. "I'm great for conversation, but you know you deserve a girl who matches your looks."

He shook his head. "I'm looking at the most attractive woman I've ever laid eyes on."

"Stop! You're just—"

"No, I'm not." He leaned forward and took my hand in his. "Do I strike you as a man who just says things to placate another? No woman compares to you, Katerina. When you leave, all I can think about is when you'll be home again. Whatever physical flaws you think you have, I don't see. Even before we met, when I imagined my ideal mate, I saw *you*."

He cupped my face with his hand, the other settling on the curve of my waist. "The same figure. Your long hair. Perhaps not every vivid detail, but I craved you. When I finally saw you in the flesh, it was like my every fantasy came true."

Tears pooled in my eyes as I listened to him. Could he possibly be telling the truth? "But I'm... I'm... bigger than..."

"Why do you assume that's ugly?" he asked softly. "Who told you that lie?"

"Everyone," I croaked out. All my life. Everyone at school, growing up. Comparing me to my perfect, younger sisters.

Every boyfriend. The media. Magazines. Society.

He didn't say a word. He simply drew me into his arms on the sofa, and I broke down into sobs. The pain of past rejection, the pressure to live up to a standard I wasn't genetically designed for, the relief and love he felt for me... it all was too much to hold onto. I released it all hile being held in his arms and sobbing against his chest. When I finally stopped sobbing and my face was wet and hot, he lifted my face toward him.

"Better?" he asked.

"Yeah." I wiped at the tears, needing to blow my nose. "I'm sorry I was a bitch."

Now I really must look ugly. "I need a tissue. Give me a minute." I jumped up and grabbed for the Kleenex box, mopping my face.

When I finally felt like I'd gotten control of myself, I sat down beside him once more.

Then Lucian leaned in and kissed me. Soft at first, but as his lips touched mine, heat exploded between us. That same hunger and need that I felt the night of Sarah's wedding. It would be so easy to just fall into that same heat and pleasure. But I was scared.

"Tell me I can trust you," I whispered against his lips. "That you aren't going to break my heart."

"You can trust me," he said softly. "I'm not going to hurt you. My word is my bond, and ours is forever."

Swoon. I pulled him in for another kiss, pressing my chest against his, ready to have him right then and there. He did something that surprised me.

He picked me up. Correction. He lifted me up into his arms and I was being held in a classic damsel-on-a-romance-cover pose. Never before in my life had any guy ever attempted such a gesture of affection, let alone achieved it so easily.

I wrapped my arms around his neck and gazed lovingly into his dark eyes. My heart was already his, completely open and vulnerable. Lucian could do whatever he wanted to me and then some—for better or worse.

I was smitten, head over heels, and it was dangerous.

Lucian carried me to the bedroom, sat on my bed, and stroked a few strands of hair out of my face. "You're breathtaking. So beautiful. Would you stand so I can see all of you?"

"I... okay." I crawled off his lap and stood in front of him, awkward and shy.

He stood with me and circled around me, studying every part of me. Slowly, he undressed me, piece by piece. First, he slipped my blouse down my arms. Then he kissed my bare shoulders so tenderly that he sent a shiver of longing down my spine. Next, he helped me out of my pants, letting them drop to the floor. A hand ran along my bare legs, and I could barely hold in the moan.

Everything he did with me, and to me, was magical.

"I'm not sure which part of you is my favorite," he confessed, his voice husky and deep. "There are so many wonderful things about your body. Your soft skin, those legs for days..." He moved behind me and kissed my neck. "You taste delicious."

I giggled to break the tension around us. "Are you a cannibal now?"

"Ha." He undid the clasp of my bra and let that fall to the ground next.

I struggled not to cover myself with my arms. The light in the room was stark. He'd see every ripple of cellulite, my sagging boobs...

Lucian moved in front of me and took my breasts in his hands, plumping them up, then dropping his head to suckle on each of my nipples.

My weight forgotten, I threaded my fingers into his beautiful, thick hair and let out a moan of pleasure.

He glanced up at me. "Oh, I love that noise you make. And the look on your face... I want to see more."

"This isn't fair," I choked out as he slid my panties down my legs and continued to kiss along my skin. "You have way too many clothes on."

"I can fix that." He stripped quickly, revealing his muscled body to me. His eagerness was clear when I saw his large cock bounce up, red and swollen.

He wants me. And, God, I want him.

Lucian sat down on the bed and laid back. "I want to watch your pleasure. If that's all right, I mean. Your face is beautiful."

He wanted me on top of him? Seriously?

I swallowed hard, nervous yet excited. No one ever wanted to see me in that position, but the fact that he did, made me trust him even more. I slid my leg over his waist and straddled his ridged abdomen.

I didn't want to hurry, so I leaned forward and trailed kisses down his sculpted chest, rocking my hips so that I could feel his large cock beneath me.

I groaned when he shifted beneath me, found my entrance and entered me. I ached for him, and his length filled me so perfectly it was hard not to sob with relief.

"That feels sooo good."

Lucian grabbed my hips and guided me into a rocking motion. I put my hands on his chest and stared down at him, the intensity in his face making every moment better.

Together, we found our rhythm, and we were even more in sync than last time. Waves of pleasure rolled over me with every thrust of his body inside mine. I gave him exactly what he wanted, letting him see my pleasure. I was exposed and free. Insecurity fled and I relished in the sensation of the depth of his want—his love.

I closed my eyes and threw my head back, riding him faster and harder. I moaned, I gasped, and told him in every way how much I wanted him.

He let me take control, let me set the pace. I glided up and down his cock over and over again, building the pleasure inside my belly.

When he groaned and grabbed for my hips, I stared down at him. His face was set, his jaw clenched. He was close.

He began to thrust up into me, amplifying my pleasure. I gasped as he pushed me closer to orgasm.

"Oh... Ah..."

Lucian fucked me hard and fast, pushing me higher. The

sensation was almost too much to bear, yet not anywhere near enough. I moved faster, needing more until we hit the peak together and climaxed. Lucian cried out and buried himself deep inside me, pulsing heat into my belly.

His orgasm pushed me into a rolling orgasm, making me scream and shudder.

I collapsed onto his chest, shivering in his arms. My orgasm continued to echo inside me, my pussy still pulsing around his cock. Lucian gently rolled us to the side, holding me close. I cuddled into his body for warmth now that the heat of the session began to dissipate.

He drew a blanket up and over us, then came back to lay his head against my chest. "Dinner will be cold now."

"That's what microwaves are for," I murmured, wrapping my arms around his shoulders and holding him to me.

"How about I go use it and bring dinner to you?" His eyes lit up, as though he was eager to serve.

I smiled at him, my post-orgasmic bliss stealing over me and making me drowsy. "Yes, please."

"I'll be right back."

I lay back in bed and closed my eyes, the whole night replaying inside my head. Once again, sex with Lucian felt like a dream.

I still couldn't believe that he'd picked me up and carried me to the bedroom. The attentive way he'd worshiped my body had been truly beautiful, and the fact that he wanted to bring me dinner in bed afterward was surreal. It all felt too good to be true.

But it *was* all real. My life wasn't just a fantasy playing out in my mind. Finally, I had the chance for a solid relationship that would go the distance.

My hand crept down and pressed against my still-flat stomach.

I also had a chance to have the family I'd always wished for.

With my child, I'd have a deep connection. I wouldn't be distant like my parents were with me when I was younger. My child would be close with aunts, and siblings who may follow.

So much potential for happiness, and all of it within my grasp. At last, life was finally turning around.

CHAPTER

TEN

Lucian

I should have been living my happily ever after.

Katerina was mine at last, and she was willing to give me a chance to show her my love and commitment. From there, we should have been planning a wedding and making her home *our* home. We should have finally been at peace.

Unfortunately, that peace didn't last. We spent the first week engrossed in each other. While she left for work during the day, I tidied up the house and repaired any broken items in her home. Her dripping kitchen sink, and the toilet that ran incessantly unless the handle was jiggled. All while cooking and tending to her basic needs, so that our evenings could be spent in bed.

Making love to her was the highlight of my day. She was luscious and generous in bed. So fucking beautiful.

Over the two days she called the weekend, we went on a date in town, and I got to see more of her neighborhood. None of it felt like home, and the way the humans lived seemed strange to me.

I wasn't sure how they felt purpose in their lives or content-ment, but I was willing to learn.

The following Monday morning, some of the glow began to fade.

"Are you sure you want to stay home alone all day?" Katerina asked while she was picking up her keys to leave for work.

I nodded, that tight feeling in my gut returning at the reminder of how out of place I was in this world. And how much I missed her when she was gone. "Where else can I go? I can't watch you work."

"No, I guess not," she mumbled. "That'd be a distraction. For me and the kids." She paused. "But you can meet them at the school social next Friday."

"I'd like that." I wanted to watch her with her students and get a taste of what she did at work.

"Great!" Her eyes lit up and her obvious excitement reduced my despondence at knowing she'd soon be gone for the day. "What are you going to do while I'm at work?" she asked.

"I'll find something around here to fix." I gave her a quick grin.

She kissed my cheek. "Thank you. I'll be back before you know it."

And then she was gone, and I was alone again. If I could find an actual purpose, then I might feel less bored and frustrated. Back in my home realm, I'd fly and patrol the lands on a regular basis to make sure it was safe from our enemies. Or I'd train. There, I felt useful and needed. Here in the human realm I was nothing.

I had to look on the bright side, though. I had Katerina. I'd figure something out. This world was new to me. I couldn't judge the place from living here for only one week. Settling in took time.

That's what Dymitri would tell me. Just give it time.

When her car disappeared from sight, the emptiness hit me

like a solid blow to the gut. I looked about the house. How could I help her next?

My gaze landed on her front yard. The space had clearly been neglected for some time. The lawn was trimmed just enough to prove someone lived at the house. Her flowers looked awfully thirsty and were obviously struggling to survive.

Her yard in back was rather sad to behold in general. She had a few potted flowers, and the tiniest of patios. Maybe she'd enjoy her backyard more if there was a beautiful space in which to spend time. That was something I could help with!

I found a blank piece of paper and began to sketch out a plan. A better patio. No, I decided. She should have a deck in the back! With a place for a nice fire pit for bonfires in the evening. The thought of cuddling up to her in front of a fire brought a smile to my face. I could make a spot for flowers along the edges. She would like that, and then I'd make her a vegetable garden.

My heart lifted as I planned and sketched. When I finished the plans, I nodded in satisfaction. Now, I just had to build the thing. Katerina had tools in her garage. Surprisingly, a lot of them. All I needed was the wood. It seemed the human realm sold wood, cut and ready for use—quite different from my home, where we had to take an axe out into the woods and chop down what we needed.

Thanks to some cash Katerina had left for me, I was able to get my order delivered within a few hours. By the time she came home, I had the wood organized in piles, along with all the other supplies needed.

She didn't notice. Her backyard was a chaotic disaster, and she didn't once glance out the windows.

When I walked inside to greet her, she yawned loudly. "Ugh, I'm exhausted. Are you okay with just cuddling on the couch tonight? I don't care what we watch. I'm just so..." She yawned again.

"Whatever you need," I said, meaning every word. "I'll make dinner for us. Go ahead and relax. Your day must have been tough."

"Those kids have too much energy. I can't keep up sometimes," she said with a tiny smile, meandering over to the couch.

I frowned, disappointed at the fact she hadn't noticed the beginning stages of my latest project. However, this created a new opportunity. If she was always tired upon coming home, which she seemed to be, then I could reveal the new deck to her once it was finished. It'd be a great surprise!

So that's what I worked on every day to pass the time—the only way I felt I could be of use to her since she always seemed so run down and tired. All the while, I pondered how I could find my place in the human world.

When Friday rolled around, I was excited for the change of scenery and to see more of Katerina's world. She drove us to her school in her car—something I didn't need at home, obviously, with my in-built wings. School turned out to be a small, brick building, buzzing with activity as every student played outside on the playground while the parents and teachers chatted. Teachers at a table handed out ice creams.

As soon as we got out of the car, lots of young children ran up, shouting for Katerina.

"Miss Kat! Miss Kat!" one girl called out. Her gaze settled on me, and her eyes widened. "Is he your boyfriend!"

Katerina gazed up at me and laughed a little self-consciously. "Something like that, yeah."

Not quite the enthusiastic response I was hoping for, but it was better than her saying "no". The realization that she was finally attaching a level of commitment to our relationship was a good thing, though.

She *did* want me. Otherwise, I reminded myself, she wouldn't have taken me here to meet her students and co-workers. That gave me hope that she wanted the future I did too.

This is going to work. We are going to be okay.

"He's really tall," a boy said, coming over. "And big! I can't see! The sun is in my eyes."

I knelt down so I was closer to his height. "Is this better?"

The boy narrowed his eyes, studying me. "I guess you're okay."

I chuckled and took Katerina's hand as the boy ran off. Her fingers closed tightly around mine, as if she was grateful for the contact. She still wasn't saying much in relation to us, but small gestures like that were becoming more frequent.

We moved toward the playground, the kids talking so fast I could barely keep up. Katerina declined the offer of an ice cream when we passed the table.

"My stomach is still feeling off," she said, putting her hand to her belly. A problem she'd been having a lot more lately. Was she ill? Maybe going out was a bad idea.

"Are you okay?" I asked, squeezing her hand.

She nodded. "I'm great. Promise." She gave me a reassuring smile, and that was enough. For the moment.

I watched my mate in her element. She talked to the students like they were her friends, and she handled all of the parents with grace—including any who talked to her about concerns they had.

Her co-workers bombarded me with all kinds of questions. Where had we met? Where was I from? How long had we been together? I tried to keep all my answers simple, as Katerina seemed to value her privacy.

"My brother's wedding... A small town. You probably haven't heard of it... It's been a few weeks."

I hoped I was doing well, but still felt like a fish out of water. I wasn't used to following someone else's lead. Seeing her with her friends and her work family... it made me miss my own. I hadn't spoken to Dymitri since leaving home weeks ago. He was honey-mooning though, so he was probably glad I wasn't there to interrupt.

I wanted to actually see him in person—taking to the skies together like we used to. The urge to let out my dragon and fly was becoming more urgent the longer I stayed here.

I assumed Dymitri was doing well. Someone would have arrived across the veil to tell me otherwise if he wasn't. And Damon... I had still been getting to know him when I left. Would our burgeoning relationship take a step backward because I wasn't home?

No, he'll understand. This is my true mate, after all.

I still missed him though, and the odd family bond we'd begun to build.

My brothers, my home, now felt like a place that only existed in my dreams. It was a feeling that left me anxious. A lot about Katerina's world did that. I was in a foreign land with only one ally.

I smiled my way through the event, being polite and keeping my grumpy dragon at bay while he screamed at me internally. For Katerina, I refused to falter. I was determined to never lose control of my shifter again.

We only stayed for an hour, but it felt an awful lot like five.

"Thank you for coming with me," she said as we climbed into the car. "But I can tell you weren't exactly comfortable there. If you hated it you don't have to come next time."

I shook my head. "I want to be with you. I'll get used to the crowds eventually. I've never been much of a people person."

"Not surprised by that at all." She laughed, turning on the engine and pulling out of the parking lot. "That brooding loner vibe you give off almost scared me away from talking to you at the wedding."

"It did?" I glanced over at her, surprised at the comment.

She squeezed the steering wheel a little tighter. "Almost, but I can't stay away from you. Even if my head tells me none of this makes sense... I feel..."

"The bond," I finished for her. "What you're feeling is our bond."

"It's definitely something," she admitted quietly, then louder she said, "I like it, though. What we have. It's different from anything I've ever experienced, and it's nice to have it all feel easy."

I nodded, showing I was listening, though I didn't necessarily feel the same way.

Being with Katerina felt safe—like home. But it was far from easy. I don't think she understood how much of my life was being changed or put on hold for her comfort. I didn't plan on telling her any time soon, though. The least I could do was try and adapt for her. She'd already done the same for me, letting me into her life. Lovers compromised for each other all the time...

Didn't they?

"When we get home, I want to show you what I've been doing all week," I said, feeling a flutter of excitement inside my chest.

"Besides cleaning my house and cooking?" she said, her eyes sparkling with light. "You know, I was starting to wonder how you didn't die of boredom. That night I said that, about doing all my cooking and stuff. I didn't mean you really had to. I was feeling pretty cranky and, well, I appreciate all you've been doing, but you don't have to."

"I want to," I said, glancing out the window as the houses flew by. And it was true. I did enjoy doing things to make Katerina's life easier if I could.

She cleared her throat. "I... err... there's something I want to talk to you about when we get home, too."

Her mouth snapped shut then, but her eyes were soft. What did she want to talk about? It didn't seem like anything to be concerned about. "Okay," I said, deciding I could be patient. "Me first, though. I really want to show you…" I broke off, nearly giving away the surprise.

"You've got me curious now," she said, and we shared a quick grin.

When we arrived, I put my hands over her eyes as soon as we were out of the car. "Trust me, I won't let you stumble."

She giggled and pressed her warm fingers over my hands. "I trust you."

I loved hearing those three words.

I guided her through the garage and to the back door. We entered the backyard, and I brought her to the edge of the new deck. "Now you can look." I removed my hands from her eyes and walked around her so I could see her reaction.

She squinted for a second, then gasped. "You… how… what?"

"This is what I made while you were at work this week."

"How did I not notice?" Her voice was full of wonder. She stepped up the small staircase and then sat on one of the built-in bench seats on the deck. "There's no way you did this all by your-self, surely?"

"Of course, I did." I sat next to her. "You didn't notice because you come home exhausted every night and you're early into bed, too."

"Do not."

I gave her a pointed look. "I've seen more brain activity from a zombie."

She gasped. "Zombies are real too?"

I snorted. "Not as far as I know. It was a joke, Kat."

A blush spread across her cheeks. "It's been a long week. And, yeah, I guess you're right. I have been extra tired, lately."

"I'm not judging you," I clarified. "Though I am worried."

She took a deep breath and let it out slowly, then whispered something almost under her breath. It was only my acute dragon hearing that managed to pick up what she'd said. "I'm afraid of losing you."

"Kat," I said, lifting a hand to stroke her cheek. She leaned into my caress and closed her eyes for a moment. "I'm not planning on going anywhere."

"I..." She took another breath in and out. "I'm good. It's just..."

"Been a long week. I know." I nodded and grabbed one of her hands with my own. "And now you have another place you can rest. Perhaps having some sunshine will help?"

"Maybe," she whispered. She bit her lip then shook her head. "Thank you, Lucian. For everything. Your patience. Everything."

I leaned in and kissed her sweetly on the lips. "I would do anything for you."

Even keep my dragon at bay.

I couldn't lose her.

For her, I'd find a way to make this strange world full of humans work.

"I don't know what I'd do without you," she whispered as she stared up at me with her big, beautiful eyes glistening with unshed tears.

Those words made the sacrifice feel worthwhile.

I wanted to tell her I loved her, to show her how deeply that love ran by taking her upstairs to bed and ravishing her until she screamed in ecstasy. Instead, I put my arm around her, settled her into my embrace, and we gazed across her fresh lawn. If the house felt like home for her, it could feel the same for me as well.

Home was a construct created by connections. My dragon family would understand.

ELEVEN

Katerina

Every time I tried to tell Lucian I was pregnant, the words stuck in my throat. At first, it was simply fear of losing him that stifled my voice. What if telling him ruined everything? We'd reached the month-long milestone in our relationship with hardly any hiccups.

Then, as time went on, I was embarrassed that I'd said nothing, and it became even harder to broach the subject. How was I going to tell him? The right words just weren't coming to me. We got along so well. Everything felt so good. So... right.

I desperately wanted to tell him, I really did. But it had been so long now, I felt stuck. Three weeks passed quickly and I remained silent. I worked with my kids and Lucian worked on projects around the house. Every day he updated something. It wouldn't have surprised me if I came home one day, and he'd decided to gut the kitchen and start fresh.

I was just glad he had found something that he seemed to enjoy.

As the weeks passed, my morning sickness grew stronger, and my exhaustion became harder to ignore. I thought for sure Lucian would put two and two together, but he didn't.

He noticed I often wasn't feeling well, but he wasn't hugely familiar with my life or that of normal humans, so I guess he assumed that tiredness was a normal condition for me. After all, we hadn't spent much time together before he'd moved in. Not to say he ignored my health, quite the opposite. He asked me often if I felt okay, and if I was sick. Not once did he ask if I was pregnant, and I still hadn't told him.

"You need to eat," I whispered to myself as I stared down at the lunch I had brought to work with me. Once again the food was going to go uneaten.

I didn't know what to do, and wanted to ask my sisters for help. But Sarah was likely busy being a new wife, and Nadia hardly answered her phone. The reception in the other realm seemed to be terrible. Though I'd been able to get through once or twice, I could barely hear her voice, and vice versa. It became easier not to even try calling, in the end.

If they knew I was in such inner turmoil, they wouldn't ignore me, of that I was sure. Part of me didn't want to say anything anyway, because I knew they'd side with Lucian. It was so easy for them to tell me not to worry. They'd never known rejection like I had.

I gazed at my lunch, wishing I could will myself to eat. So far, I'd dropped three pounds. The internet said that losing weight was normal in the beginning of a pregnancy, so I tried not to worry about the baby too much. If a human baby sucked up a lot of energy from its mom, then I imagined a half-dragon baby might deplete even more.

"I have to tell him this weekend," I mumbled to myself and rubbed at my forehead with a hand. "I've put it off long enough."

I needed to stop being a coward. Come what may, Lucian had

the right to know, and I didn't want to hide it from him any longer. I wanted him to know why I kept refusing wine with dinner, and why I wouldn't eat the sushi he'd bought. It was time, and I'd find a good way to break the news that hopefully put it in a positive light so he wouldn't run away screaming. Again.

"Tomorrow, I'm treating you for a change," I announced when I walked in the door that night after work. "So don't make any plans, okay?" That would buy me a night to think and plan.

If only he wasn't so distracting. With those lips... and the way he touched me... We made love practically every night. I didn't have a ton of energy, but I always managed to find time for that! Being one with him restored my soul in ways I'd never thought possible.

Lucian gazed at me, his head tilted slightly to the side. "Why?"

I coughed, startled. "What do you mean, why? Can't I do nice things for you too? You've been working so hard around here, and doing so much."

"Because I..." He swallowed. "All right. I won't argue."

"Good! I mean, you built me a freaking *deck*!"

"I was bored. You needed one." He shrugged like it was nothing.

It wasn't nothing, and it wasn't just the deck. He'd transformed my old, needing-some-TLC house, into a stunning place.

I shook my head. "Goof."

"That's a peculiar term of endearment," he said as he walked over and grabbed me. Then he kissed me deeply, and I melted into him. My nervousness grew and I made love to him that night like it might be the last time.

Being Friday, I didn't have to work for the next two days. That gave me plenty of time to plan, spill the beans, then deal with the fallout, whatever it might be. I slept restlessly, unsure of what the future would bring, but knowing it was time to step up and be an adult. I was going to become a mom! I needed to let

Lucian know, and then we would deal with whatever happened next.

The next morning, I rose early and went straight to the store to get everything I needed for my big announcement. A light lunch for myself and something more substantial for him. If things went well, there were cupcakes. If things got awkward fast, I had fruit salad… and I'd save the cupcakes for myself later, if I could bring myself to eat them.

I set a blanket across the lovely new deck and some pillows on the blanket to soften the seating. It seemed such a small gesture in comparison to everything he'd done for me.

"Ready for lunch?" I asked, my stomach twisting with anxiety.

"Sure," he answered, sweeping his long hair back into a low ponytail and fastening it with one of my hair ties. "What's going on, Kat?"

Instead of answering, I took his hand in mine and walked him outside. We both got comfortable on the blanket, and I sat with my legs crossed and my hands in my lap. How was I going to even start?

He looked at me expectantly, so I just rushed into the conversation. "So… your instinct was right. I do have a hidden agenda."

Oh my God, that sounds terrible!

He frowned. "Should I be worried?"

"Maybe," I mumbled. "Hopefully not." I took a deep breath, and then just blurted out the news I'd been trying—and failing—to tell him for days. "Lucian, I'm pregnant."

Not the graceful, fun way I'd wanted to tell him, but nerves had gotten the better of me.

I braced myself for the worst, watching him carefully and barely able to breathe as I tried to gauge his reaction. He said nothing. He didn't even look at me. He just stared down at one of my pretty pillows, decorated with purple lace, and blinked a few times before reaching out a finger to trace the lacy pattern.

Had he heard me? Was he in shock? Horrified? Was he about to jump to his feet, shift into his dragon form, and fly off into the sky?

"Um, anyway," I said, when the silence continued. "I started suspecting right before you decided to knock on my door. That makes me think I'm about eight weeks along now, but I'm not sure. I haven't been to a doctor or anything yet. I, uh... think it happened the night we first..."

Finally, he spoke up. "The wedding."

"Yes." I took another shuddering breath, trying desperately to keep calm. My insides were churning, and my chest was tight. This was it. This was the part where he ran. "So, I'm sorry this happened. It's not like I wanted it to be this way. And I'm sorry I didn't say anything sooner, but I wanted to be sure. That's why I've felt so unwell lately, and exhausted."

More silence.

"If this is where you want to bow out, that's fine. I won't take it personally. I know having a kid is probably not high on your to-do list. I'll deal with this alone." I swallowed back my tears as my throat began to tighten. "Don't feel like you owe me anything, Lucian. You don't. You really don't."

"What are you talking about?" he asked, finally lifting his head and gazing at me. An enormous smile formed on his lips and his eyes shone. "This is *amazing*!"

"It... it is?" I blinked, unsure if I'd heard him right. I was so sure he'd be unhappy.

Was he serious?

"Yes! Of course, it is!" He reached over and tugged me into his arms. "We're going to be parents! We've bonded and mated and now there's going to be a little one as proof of our love."

I laughed awkwardly, swallowing hard against the clog in my throat. "It's proof of something."

That we'd jumped into bed the minute we met.

"I know I love you," Lucian said firmly, staring down at me.

I struggled to sit up properly, staying close, but not wanting to be in his arms anymore. I needed space between us, so I could study his expression.

"Please don't lie to me just because I'm pregnant," I whispered. "You barely know me. How can you love me? Because some witch told you I was your soulmate? Because an inner beast insists it's true?"

Nothing about his dragon soulmate tale made any sense to me. Not any logical sense, anyway.

Lucian's eyebrows lowered and he stared at me, hard.

"We've got our whole lives to discover everything about one another." He grabbed my hand and gave it a squeeze. "What I feel is real. I hope you feel it, too. That's what matters right now. Everything else will fall into place."

Deep in my bones, I agreed with him. It did feel real. And so damn right. But that treacherous voice in the back of my head wouldn't shut up. "Things are only going to get harder, you know that, right? Kids complicate life. I'm not going to be one of those graceful, sporty, awesome moms. I feel terrible, physically. I hate how I look and that's only going to get worse as I get bigger. I'm a hot mess, Lucian."

"Yes, you are indeed hot," he purred.

"Ha." I shoved at his chest, not sure whether to laugh or burst into tears.

"I'm being very serious," he said. "Why do you keep talking so poorly of yourself? I thought we'd discussed this already."

I looked away, unable to handle the weight of his gaze. "Because it'll be easier on me if we do this now rather than further down the road. The longer you wait, the higher my hopes get, and then when you leave... it'll destroy me."

And any child we had together.

"You're planning for a day that is never going to come." He stroked my cheek with his fingers. "You have to keep trusting me."

"What if I can't?"

My biggest fear of all. What if I was too damaged by the past to ever be the woman he needed?

"Take it day by day." He pulled my face toward his, so I was looking into his eyes again. "I'm not like any of those other men." One of his hands clenched into a fist. "Just thinking about how you've been taken advantage of... that is never going to happen again!"

The flash of anger in his eyes made my breath catch in my throat. He meant every word. And that anger had flared on my behalf. He cared. He really did care.

He took in a slow breath, and his muscles tensed. "No one will hurt you or our child. I promise."

"But what if—"

"No!" Lucian growled. "There is no what if. I'm not leaving you. I'm not leaving our baby. We are bound to each other for life. Not just because of the soulmate bond, but because of that child. I am not going to abandon you, or my future son or daughter."

My heart fell. The man before me was honorable, and I adored him for that. But I wouldn't take advantage of him because of that amazing trait.

I'd never be able to live with myself if he stayed out of a misplaced sense of duty.

"Don't stay in a relationship with me simply because of the baby, either," I whispered. "Let's not lie to ourselves like that."

Another growl and I actually saw a scale form on his forearm. "I am with you because I want *you*. I always will. One day you'll begin to trust me—trust *us*—and you'll see."

I gazed at the scales developing on his skin and shivered at the growl that came from his mouth and throat. "Please," I whispered. "If you can't keep control over yourself, I'm going to need you to leave. The dragon... I can accept that it's part of who you are, but it doesn't belong in this world. It's dangerous. For me, the baby, and for you."

He'd be locked up, or worse, if anyone from here saw him transform into a dragon.

"I'm not going anywhere without you!" His chest puffed up as he spoke, and he got more animated by the second. "Just let a puny human try to take me on! They won't get far!"

"Lucian!" I gasped. "*I'm* one of those puny humans!"

He gazed at me and the fear I was feeling on the inside must have been written all over my face, because the tension left his body.

"Yes, I mean everyone else. Like the men who've hurt you in the past."

"They're not here anymore," I said. "And I don't plan on ever talking to them again."

"Good." Lucian closed his eyes and the scales disappeared until there was only tanned flesh once again. He opened his eyes, and the man was fully back. "Does my dragon scare you?" he asked.

"It can," I said honestly. "Mostly when he tries to come out uninvited. Which seems to happen a lot, according to my sister. What if you get angry and..."

He shook his head. "My dragon would never try to harm you. Or the baby."

I knew *he* believed that, but dragons were so unfamiliar to me. How did I know for sure? How did he know, if he'd never had a mate before? "Regardless, you can't do that here. You can't change."

"Yes, I realize that would complicate things," he said.

We were both quiet for a long time.

Then his dark eyes lit up and he grinned at me. "We'll go back to my realm! We can live in the castle with my brothers and your sister. There I won't have to hide who I am. I can return to a normal life. You'll be safe, and we can raise our child together." He paused. "We can be a family. A real family."

Then in a whisper he added, "Everything I've ever wanted."

It was everything I'd ever wanted, too. Being with him, raising our child together in a home we built together... it sounded magical. Perfect. Perhaps too perfect.

I remembered the grandness of the castle. I'd been in awe and intimidated all at once. As beautiful as it was, I didn't feel drawn to stay there like my sisters clearly had. Nice to visit, but not a place to make a permanent home.

I shook my head. "I can't go back there. Your home... it's so cold. It's so far from everything I love here. My students, my father. I can't give them up. That castle didn't feel like home to me."

"I see," he said, nodding slowly and showing no emotion on his face.

Was it the same for him here? Did my home not feel like, well, *home* to him? How would we reconcile the fact that we were so different—and from completely different worlds?

"I don't want to keep you from your own kind," I said. "But you can't keep me from *mine*, either. I love this place, Lucian. Do you not think you could make it your home too? I hope you'll find a way to make this work, because I'm not leaving."

I hadn't planned to have any sort of ultimatum in this conversation, but there it was. I'd laid down the gauntlet, whether I'd wanted to, or not.

Neither one of us said anything for a long time after that. I worried that maybe I'd pissed him off and succeeded at pushing him away. After all, he was a dragon. Clearly, Lucian enjoyed being tough and in charge.

At long last, he cleared his throat. "Then obviously, the solution is that I stay. I learn self-control, keep my dragon in check, and I learn how to be human."

"Really?" I had to make sure I heard him right, that my ears weren't deceiving me.

He nodded. "Yes, really. It won't be easy, but the reward will be worth it."

Wow, he did love me like he claimed. "I thought for sure…"

"Katerina, you need to believe me. I'll do anything for you." He leaned over and kissed my lips softly. "For you and our child."

For the first time, I really did believe him. He was proving it.

Guilt stung my heart as the weight of what I'd just forced onto him hit home. I'd just asked him to deny his instincts for me. To hide half of his very being—his dragon. To give up his family and everything he was familiar with. To move to a foreign world where he knew no one and had nothing else but me.

It was so much to ask… too much, really.

And yet, Lucian loved me enough to do it.

I should have been elated, but instead I felt like a horrible person. I'd just demanded he do something that I myself had just declared I would never do for him.

"I'm so sorry," I whispered. "I—"

"What are you apologizing for?" he asked, frowning. "If you feel this is the best way for us to be together, I am going to trust that instinct."

His confidence in my decision helped and I moved forward to snuggle into his arms. But the weight of this conversation was going to haunt me.

I could already tell.

TWELVE

Katerina

Time passed, and we lived together just like any other human couple. I went to work, and Lucian remodeled the bathroom to make it more efficient for me and the baby.

He continued to make my backyard gorgeous, installing a swing and building a playground. He drew up plans to fix my kitchen but hadn't gotten around to actually doing the work just yet. He seemed to enjoy construction; it was how he kept busy while I was out of the house, and when I was at home, he waited on me hand and foot.

I had mixed feelings about the latter. I loved how attentive he was to my needs and to those of our coming baby. Lucian was all in, in that regard. However, as the weeks passed, our interactions began to feel hollow. Like he was with me in body, but not in spirit. He listened to me talk but didn't say much in return.

I thought maybe he was just being broody, but then I noticed he'd had an entire shift in attitude, in general. He was very quiet.

Somehow, Lucian didn't seem like the man I'd met the night of the wedding, and I wasn't quite sure what to do about it.

I was in week sixteen of my pregnancy and feeling a lot better. Once I'd gotten out of the first trimester, my appetite had returned, and life had gotten a little easier. However, now I was growing a bump, and becoming increasingly more uncomfortable. I had no idea how to tend to Lucian's emotional needs, or what the problem even was.

He wouldn't open up to me. How did I get him to do that?

Not that I was any better. I was going to my third doctor's appointment to check in on the baby, and I didn't tell Lucian that's why I was leaving for the day—only that I had errands to run for a few hours. He hadn't gone to any of my appointments, actually.

If I told him ahead of time, I knew he'd want to come with me. For the time being, I needed to go on my own. Part of me was still trying to wrap my head around growing a baby that was only half human and I needed to process what that might mean for the pregnancy itself, and for the birth.

I went to the clinic and sat in the lobby to wait. This appointment was the big one—the sonogram. I'd get to see our baby for the first time, and I was scared. What if the baby had wings or talons? The doctor would freak out. I would freak out. It'd be a mess.

A mess that I didn't want Lucian to witness. My falling apart would hurt him, I was sure.

Hearing the heartbeat for the first time hadn't been the picturesque moment I'd thought, either. I remember listening to the rapid whooshing and bursting into tears because I'd assumed that was abnormal—that I was listening to the sounds of an alien. It took the doctor twenty minutes to talk me down, and to tell me everything was in fact, just perfect.

Every visit I was told that, actually. The baby was practically perfect. That scared me more for some reason.

I didn't want to rob Lucian of these precious moments, but I was so tired of him seeing me crying, upset, sick, or anything potentially negative. No wonder he seemed so miserable all the time. He was stuck with *me*.

"Katerina Smythe," a nurse called into the lobby. I stood, and we began the process. She checked all my standard stats, then walked me back to the ultrasound room.

I lay on the exam chair and got comfortable. Warm goo was spread over my rounded belly, and a wand placed on top. To an outsider, I probably didn't look pregnant. I noticed the difference in my stomach's structure, though. I liked seeing the evidence.

My heart was pounding, and I felt like I was going to be sick. What was I going to see on the screen? Wings? Or something more human-like?

I focused on the screen and soon an image appeared. The baby looked... like a baby.

"There are the feet," the technician explained, pointing to the little white bones.

"And there's two of them?" I asked.

She laughed. "Yup! And two hands and two eyes and a nose. Your baby looks great! Let's take some measurements."

"Oh... okay." I adjusted a little and stared at the image on the screen. Sure enough, two eyes, a nose, a mouth. So human and normal. Was I wrong? Or had I dreamed that Lucian was a dragon?

No, he'd definitely turned into a dragon, and I'd been in my sound mind when I witnessed it.

The technician measured the baby's length. "Seems to be a little bigger than usual at this point. Are you sure the conception date is right?"

"Yeah," I said. "Positive." Before that night at the wedding, it had been almost six months since my last sexual encounter.

She made a note in my file, and I tried not to worry. "Did you want to know the sex?"

"For now, can we keep it a surprise?" I asked, though I was dying to know. That decision was definitely something I wanted to include Lucian on, though it was yet another thing he and I hadn't talked about. Did we want to know, or did we want to wait? Would there be a party to reveal the news to everyone? Who would even come? His family and my sisters were all in another realm, and my dad was too unwell to attend a gender reveal event.

The technician smiled. "I'll put it in an envelope for you, and when you're ready you can look. Or not."

"Thanks," I managed, though the weight of my guilt was growing by the minute.

I should have brought him today. He would have loved to see our baby.

"We're all done! I'll leave you to get cleaned up."

I nodded, grateful there wasn't much more to the appointment, because my mind was running a million miles a minute. The whole drive home, I tried to decipher my feelings from the facts. Sometimes, the two got jumbled together.

Fact: I was pregnant and starting to get excited about becoming a mother. The more time passed, the more connected I felt to the baby. I was coming to terms with the unexpected way the baby had come into existence.

Fact: Being with Lucian made me feel wonderful. He was a great man who deserved the world.

Fact: Lucian was a dragon shifter. He could change his form, and that was a trait my baby might have as well. Not might—did. Deep down in their genetic code, Lucian's dragon would live on in my child.

A baby—kids in general—I knew what to do. Dragons? Not so much. I wouldn't be able to teach him or her how to have control over their shifting, or flying, or about fated mates and the mystery behind how that worked. In fact, there was a lot about their heritage I was still clueless about.

Would Lucian be able to teach them safely in our current home? What if the neighbors saw? What if the baby breathed fire and the house burnt down? What if... there were a lot of those questions, and they all had a similar solution.

We had to go back to Lucian's realm. Our baby needed to be with its own kind. Not the answer I wanted to face, but I made peace with the hard truth on the ride home from the doctor's surgery.

I parked the car then walked into the house, rehearsing the coming conversation in my mind. Lucian would be disappointed I'd excluded him from so much, but hopefully he'd be relieved to know that we'd be moving back to his icy land and that large and not-so-comforting castle.

I shivered just thinking about it.

When I walked inside, Lucian was in the kitchen taking measurements. When his gaze fell on me, my heart sank. Despite the smile he wore on his lips, the light didn't reach his eyes.

And his face... it had sunken in. When had he gotten so thin? Even his broad shoulders looked like a shell of their former glory. How had I missed such a dramatic transformation? Lucian wasn't just miserable living here with me... he looked like he was *dying*. The longer he denied his dragon for me, the worse his condition became.

I put my hands over my face. "My God... Lucian... I'm so sorry."

"Hmm?" he asked. "For?"

"Everything," I whispered. "I don't know what to do."

He walked over and put his arms around me. "About what, beautiful?"

"About us."

His body stiffened. "What do you mean?"

"This isn't working!" I blurted out, which was far from the

graceful speech I'd planned in the car. Lucian's obvious deterioration had snapped me into a terrible headspace. Seeing him in such a state shook me.

Lucian balked. "Again, what do you mean? I thought things were going well between us. We're not fighting. We're creating a home. Nothing has been bad!"

"Are you kidding me?" I shook my head, only just holding in my tears. "Lucian, I can see it all over your face. Your whole demeanor. Staying here is bad for you. You hate it here."

"No, I don't." He growled.

"Yes, you do!" I threw up my hands and turned away, because if I continued to study his thin face and frame, I'd break into ugly crying. "And I hate myself for doing this to you. You deserve so much better than staying here with me!"

He gasped. "Hardly. You are my true mate. You're the perfect one for me. Wherever you are, is the place I'm meant to be."

"I'm not the perfect one for you!" I snapped. "I'm *killing* you! You've lost weight. You don't look happy! You seem weak. This isn't right. None of this is okay! Stop lying to me to save my feelings and be *honest* with me for a change! How am I supposed to trust you otherwise?"

Lucian didn't respond right away. "Fine!" he said at last. "You want honesty? I'll give you honesty. You're right, I'm not happy. I'm miserable."

I cringed. Hearing the truth stung, but I also let out a breath I didn't know I'd been holding as relief washed over me. Truth. Finally. Now we were getting somewhere.

I spun back around to face him.

"I'm not happy because I feel like I'm worthless to you," he said. "Every day, you make it a point to tell me that you don't need me. That this is temporary until you determine if I meet your expectations. I work all day long trying to please you, and now it feels like you're throwing it back in my face."

"I'm not," I mumbled. "All I've asked is for a more realistic pacing. I don't want to run off and marry a guy I just met a week ago."

"It hasn't been a week. It's been—"

"Sixteen," I interjected. "Yes, I know." I patted my growing belly. "Believe me, I know."

He growled again. "Well, I didn't ask you to marry me!"

The way he said it made it sound as if he never intended to, either. "No, no you didn't."

"So I don't understand why you're so mad!"

"Because you just yelled at me for wanting something real with you." Tears fell down my cheeks. "That's all I've ever wanted. Something real. You play the part of a dutiful husband well. You take care of me physically, but you don't talk to me. You act more like you're my prisoner than anything else. And you're not."

I dared to look at him again and saw the deepest of glares. I shuddered.

"Where else am I supposed to go?" he asked. "I need to be with you and the baby to make sure you're both okay."

"No, you don't." I blinked away more tears. "We're doing just fine. The doctor said he or she is in prime health. And big." I still had the closed envelope that had the sex of the baby sealed away. "We can even find out what we're having, if you'd like to know."

I thought the news might soften him. I was wrong.

His chest puffed up. "You've seen our child? Why didn't you tell me? You're so quick to attack me for being silent, and you're keeping back just as much."

"You're right," I admitted. "Maybe this is a sign we're a bad match. We don't trust each other enough to open up and share."

Oh my God. How did this conversation turn so wrong, so quickly?

"You refuse to give me a chance." He shook his head. "Never have you said I'm your prisoner, but you treat me like one. You hint that I must remain locked away, out of sight of others, and I can't be myself. If I want to shift and let my inner dragon free, then I'm not welcome in your life. You said if I loved you, I would stay. If you loved me, you wouldn't have asked me to change who I am at my very core."

I hiccupped, sobbing. "Like I said, it's a sign. We're not good together. This was a mistake." My hand instinctively went to my stomach, and the reality hit me that I was about to be a single mother.

His eyes honed in on that gesture. "I see." He stormed out of the room, making his way to the back door.

I followed him, trying to think of anything that could possibly save what remained of our relationship. "Lucian, I'm so sorry."

I wanted to say that we'd be better in his realm. That I'd move there for him. But for some reason the words stuck in my throat and wouldn't spill forth.

"This is my fault," he ground out. "I was the one foolish enough to think the fated mate bond was real. That I could earn your love. I know now that's not how this works. You're the most incredible woman I've ever met. When you let me see your heart, it's gorgeous. I love you. I don't think you *want* me to love you, though. And that breaks me in two."

So much pain was in his dark eyes, it broke my heart to see it.

He stepped fully outside, then his body hunched forward and his skin melted into scales.

I stumbled back, both afraid and in awe of what was about to happen.

Soon, his whole body had transformed into a huge dragon. He turned his enormous head and stared at me for a few seconds, then, with a few graceful beats of his wings, he lifted into the sky. I watched him fly into the clouds and disappear from view.

I fell to my knees and broke down into sobs. The best thing to ever happen to me had just flown out of my life for good.

THIRTEEN

Lucian

"*This was a mistake.*" Katerina's words echoed in my head like a death knell as I flew away from the woman I loved.

She'd touched her stomach as she'd said it, and the message was loud and clear. Our baby wasn't wanted. *I* wasn't wanted. Everything we'd been building together these past few months was a lie. She didn't even think enough of me to invite me to that medical appointment that is one of the highlights of a pregnancy.

My anger was divided. Yes, I was mad at her for keeping so much from me. For not giving our relationship the chance it deserved. However, I also knew I could have done so much more to make her feel safe and comfortable. She didn't open up to me for a reason, and it was because I'd let her down and not opened up to her.

I'd stupidly believed that if I kept my thoughts and feelings to myself, she'd see me as patient and attentive—selfless—ready to step up and be an amazing father to our unborn child. Obviously, that wasn't the right approach, and I didn't understand what she wanted from me.

Why did I continue to get it all wrong?

You know why, I chided myself. *It's because you've never learned how to love. It's like the blind trying to lead the blind.*

That's why I'd failed so epically.

But I'd tried. I tried so damn hard. She didn't even give me an inch. Why did she still not believe me when I told her I loved her?

Leaving again was probably a mistake, but I had to get away. I had to breathe—to fly. I'd spent too much time in that house trying to make it a perfect home, and the result was destroying me. She was right about one thing—I was miserable, and I did feel trapped. I knew the only way I'd be able to think clearly would be to fly.

So, I left. And if I was honest, I wasn't sure if I'd be going back. Katerina had made it clear she didn't want me there. She was freeing me from my obligations to her and our child. Would she turn this around on me, or accept her part of the responsibility of failing as a couple?

Would she ever see that her fear of being loved—her absolute conviction that she was somehow unlovable—was breaking us before we even had a chance to be strong?

As I flew through the sky and toward the barrier between her realm and mine, I thought about my next action, which was critical. If I followed my anger, left and never returned, I'd be repeating the cycle started by my father. He abandoned Dymitri and me when we were young, and that created a hole in my heart I wouldn't wish on anyone.

But Katerina didn't want me, and continuing to stay and then fight with her would be disrespecting the wishes of my mate. Following my heart could be just as disastrous for us both. What if she hated me for being too pushy and aggressive? She could just as easily hate me for giving up.

I was damned either way.

On top of the rage, my heart ached in a way I had never experienced before. I'd just lost my mate—possibly forever. Katerina didn't love me. She thought everything we'd done together was a waste. She'd kept me from being myself, quite deliberately. No wonder I felt so off in her world. I was depressed and hadn't even realized it.

Katerina saw my misery. That has to mean something...

She had the wisdom to see that we came from two different worlds that weren't compatible. *We* were not compatible, and that put me in a state of mourning. I'd been given the chance to bond with my mate, and we'd done our duty. It hadn't worked. Now it seemed that was all we'd get in our life together.

Those moments of bliss would forever remain in my memory. I'd remember what could have been, and always regret that I couldn't figure out how to make it work. As much as I wanted to blame my father for that, I knew it was *my* problem. Dymitri made his love and his marriage work. He'd learned how to push past his trauma and pain. Me? Not so much. It took a lot to ruin things with a soulmate. We were supposed to be perfect for one another.

But I'd managed to destroy any hope of happiness for both of us.

I crossed through to my realm, a shiver of cold passing over my skin. I was home.

I considered going straight to Damon's castle to speak with him about my situation. If he had advice or insight that could change my fate, I'd gladly take it.

However, there was the possibility that he'd call me an idiot, have no wisdom left to share, and tell me that I was a lost cause.

The ridicule could wait. I needed solitude and a place to properly vent my feelings so I didn't destroy the castle I'd spent so much time repairing. Besides, I felt more at home in the quietness of the woods than I did in the grandness of the castle. I wasn't the kind of man who needed luxury. I only stayed to be close to my brother and build my relationship with my family. We were stronger together.

Without them, I'm not sure I could hold myself together.

I turned in the direction of the rudimentary house I'd spent most of my life living in. Dark, ominous clouds hung over the forest. Lightning streaked the sky. I paused to assess, slowly flapping my tired wings. The weather seemed like some kind of sign from the divine, begging me to turn around and go back to Katerina. *"Make it work,"* the rumbles of thunder urged. A request I ignored.

There wasn't another settlement to land in nearby. I could cut through the storm to the house with minimal damage, or I could take the long way around and go to the castle after all. The thought of talking to either of my brothers before I felt ready was enough to make me scowl at that option. It was just a thunderstorm. Those were common. I'd flown through plenty of them before.

Forward was my choice, as I entered the thick, billowing clouds. The wind tossed me, and the rain stung as it battered my scales at full force. I welcomed the pain. It gave me plenty of distraction from the torture inside my heart. All I wanted to do was get back to the house and wallow in peace.

A sudden gust of wind gripped my wings, causing my whole body to tip and lose balance in the air current. The storm was stronger than I'd realized, but I was confident I could handle things.

Then the hail started to pelt my body. Small orbs of ice at first, that rapidly grew in size. They hit me so hard and so fast, they began to rip my skin. One tore through the softer flesh of my right wing and I screamed with surprise at the searing fire that came with the tear. Lightning flashed in front of me, and I had only a second to try and dodge it. Without the stability of two full wings,

I lost control and tumbled backward through the sky with another surge of wind.

I rolled end over end through the clouds and toward the ground. The trees quickly came into view. If I didn't do something fast, I was going to crash land.

With a grunt and a growl, I managed to rightd myself again. My wing hurt so badly, the area was starting to go numb from the pain. More hail slammed into my body, the rain falling so hard that it might as well have been knives. This was much harder than it had ever been before. By neglecting my dragon for so long, being in that form felt foreign and weak. I didn't have the same instincts or the same strength that I'd had before I left my realm.

Lightning flashed, and this time I wasn't quick enough to evade. Flying into the storm had been a mistake, and it was one I would pay for dearly.

Electricity coursed through my system as a huge jolt of pain seared my whole body. The smell of burning flesh and smoke mixed in my nostrils. My vision blurred, and I spiraled toward the earth. I had just enough strength to flap my wings and push myself over the treetops and onto a nearby open field.

The top branches of one of the forest trees grazed my belly as I barely missed crashing into them. I landed hard on the ground, dirt and crops spraying everywhere as I rolled and eventually came to a stop.

I closed my eyes, feeling sick. My head... no, my entire body... throbbed with every beat of my heart. Spots of light lit my vision. I was so dizzy. Lightheaded, almost. Like I was floating.

Is this how it ends? Katerina, I'm so sorry. I shouldn't have left you and our child.

The lights disappeared, and the world went dark...

"We've got to get him to transform," someone said, the voice sounding distant. "It's the only way we can get him back to the castle."

"He's unconscious," another said with an annoyed tone. "How do you expect him to do that?"

Someone stroked my snout. "Wake up, Your Majesty. We need you to wake up!"

I groaned as my body coursed with pain.

"I told you he was alive!" the first person said. It was a man. "Your Majesty, we need you to turn back into a human. We can't carry you, in your dragon form."

Nothing he said made sense to me. I roared and tried to push him away, my dragon instincts taking over. The dragon wanted to flee, to lick his wounds alone. Every movement I made only increased the terrible agony. That was a good sign, I supposed. Before, I'd been feeling cold and numb. If I could feel pain and discomfort, then perhaps I'd live to see another day.

Live to try and make things right with Katerina.

Eventually, what they were saying began to make some sense. They wanted to move me, but as a dragon I was too large for them.

Turning back into a human, however, might be more of a challenge. But I had to try. I did my best to block out the pain and focus on my human shape. The familiar sensation of shifting fell over me, but it didn't last long. I reverted back to my dragon form almost immediately.

I was too weak to change.

"We could try and take him back to the castle on my cart," the second voice said, a woman. "They can help him more there than we can. And he might fit. Just." She touched my scales with a gentle hand. "Hold on, Your Majesty."

They manoeuvered a cart next to me, and somehow, with their guiding hands, I managed to lift up enough that they could roll me onto the vehicle. Though the anguish that ripped through my body at the movements was strong enough to make me pass out once more.

When I awoke, I was being transported in the cart. I barely fit, but it would suffice for travel. The storm continued to rumble overhead, though the worst of it had now passed.

I must have blacked out again because the next moment, a sharp jolt woke me. I was still in the cart. When my vision focused, I could see the gates of Damon's castle in front of us. My brothers were at my side, walking beside the cart.

"Thank God you were there to find him," Dymitri said.

"Lucian," Damon said. "Can you hear me? Do you understand where you are?"

I groaned in response, wanting them to know I did, but I couldn't shift back to tell them so.

"Here, this is for your help," Sarah said at the gate, offering the people who'd helped me something. I couldn't see.

"No, we don't need—"

"I insist," Sarah said, and that was the last I heard of her voice.

They brought me inside the castle grounds, and then multiple hands were on my scales and I was eventually inside the warmth of the palace itself. As soon as the huge front doors closed, something that felt like a soft cloud settled over my skin. Some kind of blanket? I was carried into one of the large dens and laid on a rug.

Dymitri rubbed my body with his hands, trying to warm me. "We need you to turn back into a human, brother."

"Then we can help you more," Damon said. He put another thick blanket over me. The extra heat helped to wake me up. Being cold always made me sleepy.

With the warmth, some of my strength returned. I tried once more to become human, and this time the transformation stuck. I shivered beneath the blankets, still wet and injured from my attempted journey through the storm.

"What are you doing here?" Dymitri asked. "Is everything okay?"

"Katerina…" Her name was the only word I could manage. My

head hurt and my heart pounded fiercely despite its ache. Why was it so cold? I couldn't stop shivering.

Damon put a hand to my forehead. "He's burning up. We need to get him into bed."

I tried to stand on the rug beneath me, but my legs wouldn't hold my weight. My brothers each put an arm around my shoulders, holding me up between them.

"We've got you," Dymitri said. "You're going to be okay now."

"Kat..." I tried again.

"Is she in trouble? Is that why you rushed back here?" Dymitri asked.

I shook my head, wanting to tell him all about how she didn't want me anymore. Perhaps he could see it in my eyes, because his expression changed from worry to grief.

He sighed. "You need rest, then everything will be better."

I wanted to argue with him. Nothing would ever be okay again. Instead, I blacked out once more.

The next time I opened my eyes, I was in my own room, wrapped tightly in blankets, a moist cloth resting on my forehead.

"I'm not sure the fever is breaking," Sarah said, her voice just above a whisper.

Dymitri sighed. "I'm worried. He shouldn't be this sick. This isn't normal."

"The farmers said they saw him get struck by lightning. It's a miracle he's even alive!"

"His injuries mixed with the cold... it made him vulnerable. He might have pneumonia."

Sarah took in a slow breath. "We need to get Katerina here."

"We don't know why he returned home in the first place," Dymitri said. "What if there's a problem? She's not in danger, but something happened. I think it has to do with her. He keeps saying her name, even when he's not conscious."

"All the more reason to get her here *now*," Sarah insisted. "They need to be together. It's the only way he's going to recover."

I wanted to tell them both to leave Katerina alone. She'd been hurt enough because of me. But I was too tired, too cold. I couldn't fight them.

Dymitri let out a heavy breath. "I'll go get her. Tell Lucian to hang on."

"Be careful," Sarah said. I heard them kiss. A few seconds later, she moved her hand under the blankets to hold mine. "Hear that? Hang on., Lucian. Katerina is coming. Hold on for her."

Her and the baby.

Yes... I would do that.

I think I nodded. And then I drifted away once more.

FOURTEEN

Katerina

I don't know how long I cried after Lucian left.

I didn't move from where I'd fallen to my knees. There was a vain hope running through my mind that maybe he'd return to me. And yet, I knew full well he wouldn't. Last time he left, it had been two weeks before he had the courage to come back. This time, he had no reason to return... beyond the baby, of course. But I'd made it pretty clear I didn't want him around, even though that was totally wrong. Of course, I wanted him. I loved him! Everything was a huge mess now, and it was all because of me.

Had I ever told him how I felt? No. I hadn't, and now maybe he would never know that someone loved him in return.

My fault, my brain kept taunting, over and over.

Why did I do this kind of thing to myself? Something good came my way, and I pushed it aside because I was too scared of being dumped later.

He was right. I had pushed away first. Why the hell would

anyone stick around when they weren't wanted? The answer was, they wouldn't. Could I truly be upset with him for leaving? How could I possibly fix this?

My hands cradled my stomach. "I'm so sorry, little one. It's my fault you're not going to know who your dad is. It's my fault you're not going to have a solid home like I'd been hoping. It's all my fault."

I sat there on the deck until I felt completely hollow inside. How could I not feel empty? My true love had just left my life.

My true love.

I still didn't believe in the "fated mates" concept, but there was no denying that Lucian was my perfect other half. He might have flaws, but so what? I had plenty of my own.

The way he complimented my personality was unparalleled, and the way I missed him now that he was gone was devastating. This went beyond him being the father of my baby. Even without the child growing in my stomach, I'd miss Lucian like I'd miss breathing air. I wasn't sure how to live without him.

I'd get by if I had to. And I did have to. I was responsible for another life, now. There was more at stake than just my own happiness. But my life would never be complete.

I'd always feel hollow and like a piece of me had died if Lucian didn't come back to me.

I should have been calmer when speaking with him, had more patience and been clear about my intentions. When I'd left the doctor, the plan hadn't been to push him out of my life and go solo.

I wanted him to be happy, and it was obvious he wasn't happy with *me.*

We'd both come to the same conclusion. He didn't belong in my world, and denying his true self was making him a husk of the man I'd known.

Hot tears blurred my vision as I gulped in air. I'd let my insecurities get the better of me.

I'd been so blind. I had to speak to him, somehow. But how did I find him to apologize?

"I could call Sarah," I said, thinking aloud. "She's married to his brother."

If I could tell him I was sorry, then maybe we could at least find a way to move forward for the baby's sake. Some sort of connection with Lucian was better than nothing.

But the cell phone reception between realms was crap, barely there at all, and when I'd tried to contact Nadia a few weeks ago I'd gotten the merest hint of a word here or there, and then nothing.

Not enough to provide a heartfelt apology to Lucian, that was for sure.

Damn it.

There was too much about that world I didn't understand. Why did I waste so much of my time with Lucian ignoring that part of him? I could have quizzed him about his world, and learned everything about it.

I would have been in a much better position now if I had.

I rubbed my stomach, feeling my strength return. I had a plan. "Don't be like me, kiddo. I should have asked him more questions and gotten to know him better. Magic is real. Dragons exist. You're one of them, and I never want you to feel like that is wrong."

I could at least do better with my child. I *would*. It'd be a small way I could atone for my sins against Lucian.

Finally I got to my feet, opening the back door and walking into the living room. There I swayed, exhausted. I was just about to lay down in bed so I could wallow some more, when I heard a male voice shouting my name from outside. "Katerina!"

"Lucian?" I called back, my heart in my throat.

It sounded enough like him. Maybe he was learning from his past too! Maybe he had no plans to stay away, after all. Maybe he was ready to talk and...

I ran to the front door and yanked it open. Not Lucian, but Dymitri. My sister's husband stood on the porch. He was shirtless, but blessedly wore a pair of jeans. God knew where he'd gotten them from, but I was grateful he wasn't naked.

He gazed about, frantic. "Katerina, thank God you're home!"

"What's wrong? Is Sarah okay?" The panic in his eyes said it all. Something bad had happened.

He shook his head. "It's Lucian. He..." He heaved a few heavy breaths. It was clear he'd flown a long way, and at speed.

I ran inside to get him a glass of water, my heart pounding. What had he meant about Lucian? "Come in!"

Once he stepped inside and closed the door, I handed him the drink. "Here. Now tell me. Lucian. He's okay, right?"

Dymitri gulped it down, shaking his head, and my stomach lurched. "Lucian is injured. No, sick. Well, actually, he's both."

"What do you mean he's injured *and* sick?" I demanded. I'd seen him an hour ago. Or was it more? I couldn't tell now how long I'd sat on the decking.

"He flew home, and some farmers found him. They said they saw him get struck by lightning in a storm, and he fell out of the sky."

My hand went to my chest. "Oh, God. Is he... is he..."

No. He couldn't die. Not now. Not after everything I'd said to him.

He fell out of the sky.

"He's alive? He has to be." My voice was a mere whisper.

"He is, for now. But for how long, I don't know," Dymitri said. "Our dragon forms are strong. We can withstand many things. Lucian doesn't seem to be at his full strength, though. His body seemed to recover from most of the injuries, but he has an awful fever. I think he's exerted too much of himself to heal and it's left him susceptible to illness."

I shook my head. He *had* to be okay. "Lucian is strong. He's the toughest guy I've ever met."

"Normally, I'd agree, but the man lying in his bed is..." He closed his eyes. "That's not the brother I'm familiar with."

"It's my fault." My voice cracked on the words.

"Hmm?"

I brushed hot tears away from my eyes. "It's my fault. He's been living his life here as a human. I've been making him ignore his dragon side. We got into a fight and... and..."

"That fills in a few gaps." Dymitri walked over and put his hands on my shoulders. "Dwelling on our mistakes won't fix our future. What matters is what you choose to do next."

I nodded, amazed at how gracious and kind he was being even though I'd basically admitted to killing his brother.

"I need you to come back to the castle with me," Dymitri said, his voice steady and calm. "If you return and show him how sorry you are, then it might give him the courage and the will to keep fighting."

That sounded too easy. Could it be? Would Lucian so easily forgive me? I'd only scraped the surface of our problems in my couple of sentences summarizing our issues. I'd done so much more than keep Lucian from turning into a dragon. I'd destroyed him. And his beautiful soul.

I didn't want to tell Dymitri about the baby. Not yet. My sister needed to know before him, and she needed to hear about it from my lips. Lucian would want to share the news with his brother, most likely. Who was I to rob him of that experience?

Not after I'd already taken so much from him already.

"Please, Katerina," Dymitri begged. "I'll take you back. Things can be made right again."

So much hope shone in his eyes. "Do you really think my presence will help him get better?"

"I think you're the only one who can save him." His voice was so quiet, so shaky. He was genuinely scared.

Lucian might die.

My heart thumped madly at the thought. Suddenly, I couldn't wait to get moving. "Let me pack some stuff. I'll be quick. But I'm going to need more than just the clothes on my back. If he's sick, this might be a long game."

Not to mention the fact that it was freaking freezing where he lived!

"Yes, good thinking." The worry on Dymitri's face shifted to relief. "I'll drink some more water while you pack and get myself hydrated for the journey back."

"Do whatever you need. My house is yours. We're family now, right?" I gave him a quavering smile.

He nodded, and after a moment, smiled back.

"I'll be ready in a flash." I hurried to my room and quickly packed a bag with winter-appropriate wear. It was always cold in Lucian's realm, and I hadn't been prepared for that last visit. Extra layers would be good.

I also packed my doctor-ordered vitamins and some other medical supplies. While Lucian's realm had witches and magic, I wasn't sure if there was a need for modern medicine. Silly, I suppose, but it made me feel useful and like I could make a difference.

That, right there, was part of the problem, I guess. Lucian was a dragon and from a world of magic, mystery, and things I'd only dreamed of. I was an ordinary woman from an ordinary world. I thought that by making him a part of my world—by making him more ordinary and ignoring the scaly elephant in the room—that we'd fit together better. That I could force it to make sense. But I couldn't.

The idea had only made things worse and now Lucian was paying the ultimate price.

I wasn't sure my presence really would make a difference. In fact, I was positive all I would do was take up space and get in the way. But I'd do my best, both to support him, and to earn that title of soulmate that he claimed belonged to me.

A title I'd never thought I'd hold in anyone's heart, and one I'd certainly never tried to live up to. Until now.

So much didn't make sense, but I'd made everything a mess. It was on me to clean it up and put things right. Even if we didn't end up together, I didn't want our child not knowing who his father was.

If Lucian died because of my selfishness, that was a weight I wouldn't be able to carry. How would I ever explain that to our son or daughter?

I hesitated and looked over at the envelope that contained the sex of the baby. Did I bring it along? Did I ruin the surprise? What if Lucian didn't make it? He could at least know what his future child was before he moved on. I hated the thought, but if life had taught me anything, it was to always prepare for the worst.

I packed the envelope into the bag, tucking it deep under my clothes for safekeeping, just in case.

We're not going to need to open it, though. Not unless you tell me you want to know.

A silent prayer, and I hoped whatever greater power existed heard it.

With my bag packed and the cloak I'd borrowed from the other realm wrapped around me, I went back to the kitchen to find Dymitri. He'd replenished with more water and whatever he could find in my refrigerator. Together, we cleaned up the small mess, and I locked up the house. Would I ever walk back through these doors? It might be a long time.

I hoped I'd return at some stage, and I hoped Lucian would be with me when I did. This place wouldn't feel like home without him.

"Let's go," I said.

I climbed onto Dymitri's back, closed my eyes, held on tight, and flew with him to the other realm.

Dymitri flew harder and faster than Damon had. Talk about a rush! As scary as it was, I also enjoyed the ride. I wondered what it would be like to fly on Lucian's back...

We landed near the snow-covered castle and Sarah was waiting for us in the foyer of the castle. She hugged me tightly.

"I'm so glad you came back," she whispered. "I think you're the only one who can help him."

I pulled back and nodded. "Take me to him."

Together we hurried up the stairs to his room. There, lying on the bed we'd once made love in, was Lucian. His eyes were squeezed shut, like he was looking away from something terrifying. Sweat beaded his face yet his entire body shivered under the heavy blankets wrapped over his body.

My heart thudded in my chest at the sight. I rushed over to him and placed a hand on his forehead. "He feels like fire."

And he did. He was boiling hot to the touch.

"It's bad," Sarah whispered. "I'm not sure what the actual temperature is, but I'm worried."

I pulled out the heat-sensing thermometer that I'd brought with me and ran it over his forehead, then gasped at the number. "One-oh-seven point four."

Any human would be almost dead with a temp like that.

"Do you think it's too late for him?" Sarah asked.

"I'm not sure what's normal for his kind," I said. "He's still here, and he's still fighting. That's a sign. We're not giving up." I gazed down at Lucian. "You hear that? We're not giving up!"

His body shivered. "Katerina... the forest... we..."

"Tell me all about it later," I said. "I can't wait to hear it when you're better."

"Father..." he grumbled.

I placed a hand on his chest, wanting to comfort him. His body seemed to ease at my touch. A step in the right direction. "Lucian, I'm here for you. Please rest now, and we can talk when you're better. You're not going to get well unless you rest."

His eyes remained closed, but they weren't so tightly pressed together. The crinkles and creases in his face disappeared and his breathing became more even. Deep and slow.

Dymitri was right, my presence was making a difference.

I leant over him and pressed a gentle kiss to his hot forehead. "I'm not going anywhere," I whispered against his skin. "Promise. Hold on so you can meet..."

I sighed and glanced over at my sister, but she was folding linens in the corner of the room.

"Just hold on," I said instead.

For now, that would have to be good enough. I got comfortable by Lucian's side and settled into the chair beside the bed.

I was going to be here for the long haul.

FIFTEEN

Katerina

Over the next two days, I didn't leave Lucian's side unless absolutely necessary. I ate my meals by his bed, and I slept on an extra mattress in the room on the floor beside him. I was still pretty tired from being pregnant. Exhausted in body, but with not much else to do beyond being worried, I was also a little bored.

The general consensus for Lucian's illness was some kind of mystery virus that had gotten to him in his exhausted state. Everyone agreed he was lucky to be alive.

I dressed in loose clothing to hide the small bump growing in my belly. I'm not sure how obvious it was to outsiders, but to me, it felt like the whole world could see what was going on. No one said anything about it, though, so I knew it must all be in my head.

They didn't notice I wasn't quite eating as much as usual at breakfast or lunch. While most of my morning sickness was gone, my appetite had definitely been affected by the pregnancy.

I hadn't entered the glowing portion of pregnancy, nor that moment where I could eat whatever I wanted. Certain foods still turned me off—certain smells, too. Cooking meat especially, and dragons loved their roasted meat.

"Any ideas on how I can tell your brother to not make his food so rich in flavor?" I asked Lucian one afternoon. I often talked to him, even though he didn't answer, so he would know he wasn't alone.

I sighed. "Some of his cooking doesn't make the baby happy. I haven't told him about our kiddo yet. I thought you'd like that honor, so I need to find a way to tell him that I can't eat the rich food without insulting him. Because it's not bad food. It just… isn't sitting right with me. You know?"

I waited to see if maybe Lucian would answer this time. He didn't even stir, just continued to sleep soundly. At least he looked peaceful when he slept. When I'd first arrived, his face had often contorted into anguish. Now he fought his virus in peace and hopefully some measure of comfort.

We'd managed to drop the fever down to a lower one hundred point three. And there it had stayed. Lucian wouldn't open his eyes, though. I didn't know what to think, but it had only been two and a half days. My mother always said that sleep was the best weapon against sickness.

But I did worry. A lot.

"I guess I'll have to get to know him on my own and find a good way to ask him," I mumbled. "Though, I'm sure Sarah would have plenty of tips. I hate bothering her with anything."

"You shouldn't," Sarah said quietly from the doorway. She bit her lip and walked further into the room. "Sorry, I shouldn't have interrupted, let alone eavesdropped."

"How much did you hear?" I asked.

She walked over and put a hand on my shoulder. "Not a whole lot. Just that I might have tips on something?"

"Talking to your husband," I said. "I can't eat what he's been making."

"Yeah?" Sarah raised an eyebrow.

"Uh... yeah... it's a little too rich."

Hopefully Sarah would assume it was some kind of diet fad. I prepared myself for her speech on how I was beautiful and didn't need to worry about my weight or figure.

I always hated hearing it come from her because I didn't think she'd ever understand.

But it was a speech that never came.

"Because of the baby, right?" she asked instead.

I tilted my head to the side and my mouth dropped open. "You knew?"

"As soon as you came into the castle!" She squeezed my shoulder. "And I'm so happy for you!"

"How?" I asked, still floored.

"Your bump is not discreet," she said with a huge grin on her face. "And you're absolutely radiant!"

So, I was glowing... and no one was looking at me like I was just getting extra fat? They'd figured it out?

I closed my eyes and let out a breath, relief washing over me. "My pregnancy is another of the reasons we fought."

Sarah pulled another chair from its place against the wall and dragged it over to Lucian's bedside. "Tell me everything, Kat. Start from when he showed up on your doorstep, because I want to hear it all."

I nodded and readied myself to spill everything. "Okay, well... When he first arrived, I was surprised but excited. We'd had a... uh... really good night together at your wedding." I coughed, my cheeks growing warm with embarrassment. "Don't get me wrong, the dragon thing scared the crap out of me, but... we'd connected on so many levels. He lived with me for a few months, and I introduced him to my students. I showed him normal, boring, human life."

Sarah's eyebrows flicked up. "Did the two of you get along well?"

"Yes. He wanted to come back here with me, and I told him I wouldn't go." I sighed. "Because this world…it doesn't feel like home." I gestured at the castle. "Not quite my style. I'm not a fairytale princess."

Sarah opened her mouth, then closed it and sighed.

"I'm not," I repeated. "And it has nothing to do with how I look. The way I live doesn't mesh well with it either. Anyway, what I didn't realize was that in telling him I couldn't live in his realm, I forced him into my life which didn't suit him at all. That's what started the fight."

"He didn't like it?" she asked.

I shook my head. "He didn't complain or anything. It was me that told him I hated seeing him so miserable. I told him he should leave. I hadn't meant for it to come out the way it did, but we were both heated, and I was so tired. Not just physically, but tired of everything. He wasn't talking to me anymore. We weren't bonding. He looked miserable, and he was losing weight. I just knew I was the problem."

"Kat…" Sarah shook her head. "I highly doubt that was it."

"It was." I blinked away a few tears. "He fixed my house and did all the dutiful husband things without even having the title. Perfect on paper. His soul was missing, though. I saw the empty vessel I made him. Shouldn't I be making him feel complete? That's what a soulmate is supposed to do, right?"

"Were you hiding your true self from him too?" she asked.

Not the question I was expecting.

I had to think about that one for a moment. "Kind of. He said I was pushing him away, and I can't argue with that. I was. I'm scared of letting him get to know me properly. When I let the walls down, that's when guys leave."

"Lucian isn't like other guys, though. He's your fated mate," Sarah insisted.

"And that means nothing to me!" I snapped. "A magic bond that automatically makes us perfect for each other? Seriously? He loves me because of a mystical force? How is that real?" I thought she, of all people, would understand. "I want him to love me for me."

"He does." Sarah gazed over at Lucian's sleeping form. "If you asked him right now, he would say so himself. That he doesn't love you because of magic."

"How are you so sure?"

"Because the fated mate bond... it doesn't..." She pressed her lips together. "I'm trying to think of how to explain this. It's an attraction, right? Like the moment he first walks into the room, you feel complete, but you don't know why. How you just knew you had to talk to him. It's a force that puts the two of you together, sure. But it doesn't make the love happen. That's you."

I nodded, listening, wanting to believe. "Yeah, I did feel that way. Sort of. Maybe not so strong? Not at first. That came later when he was at the house. Like when he left after our fight. I felt it the worst then... the disconnect, I mean. Like part of my soul had just been severed."

"Right!" Sarah gave me a warm smile. "With the dragons, they feel these sensations at an amplified level. The fated mate bond pulls the two of you together because it knows that you are every-thing he'd ever want in a mate. Personality, sex appeal, all of it."

I scoffed. "Right, I'm so sexy."

"You are!"

"Have you seen him, though? He's gorgeous." I pinched the bridge of my nose. "In ways that I don't compare."

"Why do you assume that?" she asked, frowning. "Because I

think the two of you look hot together. You get him to shine in ways I'd never seen. *You.* You bring that out of him! He didn't look anywhere near as good with Nadia whenever I saw them together. When Dymitri thought they were a thing, I didn't really see it."

"Nadia," I mumbled. "That makes things weird."

"Nothing happened, though," Sarah said.

I shook my head. "But he thought they were supposed to be together. Did he act all smitten with her like he did me? And then when he learned she wasn't the one, he turned it off?"

She laughed. "That's not how it went down. He knew the moment he saw her that she wasn't the one. It made him so upset he destroyed the castle. Didn't he tell you that story?"

"A version of it," I mumbled. "So, he didn't even... try? To make things work, I mean."

"Nope." Sarah shook her head. "He took care of her while she was sick." She motioned to Lucian in the bed. "Similar to this, actually. The moment she woke up and looked at him, he got all rough and grumpy. They were like oil and water."

Hearing it from Sarah made the doubt fade further. As much as I'd wanted to believe Lucian when he said it, I'd been lied to so much in the past. A few bad apples really did spoil the bunch.

But Lucian had never lied or led me astray.

I put my head in my hands. "What's wrong with me? Why can't I just trust him?"

"Why do you think you're not worthy of love?" Sarah countered. "And don't say it's because you're fat. Please. I hate hearing that kind of talk."

"Fat isn't a bad word," I grumbled. It was just... true.

"No, but saying you don't deserve love because of something so petty? That's negative thinking and unjust. Your appearance has nothing to do with your heart. So why?" She folded her arms in front of her chest.

I had no arguments. "Because no one has wanted to before, I guess."

"Lucian does."

"And I realize that now, but I've messed things up so badly."

"You can still fix it," Sarah insisted. "He's listening. Tell him what you need him to know."

I gazed over at him. "I need him to know that I do love him for him. Even the dragon side. It's a beautiful piece of his soul, even if he's rough and grumpy..,"

Sarah giggled. "Yes, he's definitely that. I promise he's a great guy, though." She paused. "Did I ever tell you about how he saved Nadia and me from kidnappers?"

"No!" I blinked. "You told me Dymitri rescued you from something bad, but... what? When were you kidnapped?"

"A few weeks before I married Dymitri." She looked down at the ground. "It's a long story. Dymitri and Lucian saw we were in trouble, and Lucian saved us, regardless. His heart is good. Pure. He does what is right and true. That's why I find it so funny you think him capable of lying. I don't think he's capable of it. He'll always be honest and pure like that. Even when you don't want him to be."

I soaked in her words. "You know, you're right. I don't know why I didn't see it before."

"You were scared."

"I was..." I sighed. "I am. I'm terrified. And pregnant."

"So I've seen."

"Does Dymitri know?" I asked.

She shook her head. "He's clueless. I didn't want to say anything before talking to you."

"Thanks. I thought Lucian might want to tell him."

"I think that'll be perfect."

Lucian groaned in the bed and his body stirred.

"It looks like this release of negativity has done some good things," Sarah said.

I put a hand to his forehead. "He feels much cooler."

"Stay with him." Sarah stood. "And I'll let Dymitri know to change up the menu."

"Thanks." I got up to hug her. "I love you."

"Love you too." She left me alone with Lucian.

I gazed over at him and grabbed his hand. "You need to wake up soon so you can spill the beans. I'm not sure how much longer Sarah is going to be able to keep it in now that she's got the news confirmed."

I kissed his knuckles. "More importantly, I need you. I want you. I always have. You've always been enough for me. Get better. We won't be able to be happy without you."

I lay my head down on his chest, then I lifted my legs onto the bed and lay down properly beside him. The rise and fall of his breathing lulled me into a slumber.

SIXTEEN

Lucian

I was plagued by the strangest of dreams. Katerina would walk over to me and slap me before telling me she was leaving me for a human. Then she said that the dragon in me scared her, and then I would change into my dragon and lose all control. I decimated the castle and the town, killing everyone I knew and loved before coming talon to talon with my father.

Then the dream would start over again. And again. And again. Constantly on repeat and showing me the parts of myself I despised the most. I couldn't escape. I was trapped in Hell.

Until one day, the dream changed. Katerina walked over to me like she always did. She raised her hand and I prepared myself for the slap. Only this time, she stroked my cheek.

"I need you," she said. "I want you. I always have. You've always been enough for me. Get better. We won't be able to be happy without you."

I pulled her in for a kiss, deep and passionate. Then the world faded to black, and I drifted off. When I did it this time, it felt more like flying. I was going home. I could feel it.

My eyes opened briefly. Katerina lay in my arms, sleeping soundly with her head resting on my chest. I tried to lift a hand to stroke her hair, but I was too weak to move.

Despite my frailness, I felt whole again, and safe.

I drifted off to sleep again, but for the first time I was not plagued by either nightmares or disturbing dreams. I simply slept, and when I opened my eyes next, Katerina wasn't in view. I stretched my arms and legs, and the movement felt refreshing—energizing! My muscles rejoiced, ready to do more than just lie in bed.

I yawned and let out a contented groan.

Katerina's face appeared out of nowhere. It took me a second to realize she had been in the room the whole time and had actually been lying on a mattress on the floor.

"You're awake!" She jumped up and hurried to my side. "You're okay!"

"Yes," I said. She grabbed my hands in her own and gave them a squeeze. Such a drastic change from the last time we'd seen each other. "I'm more than okay. I'm great."

"Yeah? You don't feel sick anymore?"

I frowned. "A bit tired, I suppose, but otherwise the same as always."

"It's like a miracle," she whispered. Louder she said, "We weren't sure if you were going to live or die. When I got here, your fever was so high, and you were delusional. Kept saying my name and something about your father and the woods. It didn't make sense to anyone."

"I was that far gone?" I asked. "The last thing I remember is being in a storm. I was hit by the elements. Wind, hail, lightning. I crashed." I frowned. "From there things start to get hazy."

She stroked my cheek with her fingers. "Yeah? Well what

matters now is that you're better. We were able to get your fever down, and now you're awake. It's been about three days total."

"That long?"

"You were very ill."

"Apparently." I chuckled, glad to be alive.

"I was so worried," she said, her eyes filling with tears. "Dymitri came to my house and told me what happened. I had to be here. I needed you to wake up so I could... I could..."

I gazed at her, worried she was about to break up with me all over again. "You could?"

"Apologize." Tears fell down her cheeks. "I was wrong to push you away. It's not okay for me to dump the baggage of my past on your shoulders to carry. Just because others have hurt me doesn't mean you will too. I should have told you about the appointment to see the baby. You're his or her father! However much involvement you want, that's what you're going to have. That's how it always should be."

Her words touched my heart, but I wanted so much more. "I want to be a part of it all. Every check-up. Every diaper. The works."

I couldn't help but start grinning. Had I really just said I'd be happy to change diapers? What had come over me?

"There's more," she said. "I'm sorry I tried to get you to deny yourself. That I pushed you into a cell and put the chains around your neck. It was so unfair of me. Your dragon is just a much a part of you as the man. I had no right to ask you to deny your own soul. Please forgive me, Lucian."

I struggled to sit up and she hurried to plump the pillows behind me.

"I do forgive you," I said, finally sitting up. I grabbed her hand. "You talk about making me carry your baggage. I've done the same to you. It's why I keep leaving instead of staying to fight. I'm afraid of fighting. I'm afraid of losing control. I don't want to be like my father."

"I'd like to work on it with you. If you can help me open up, maybe I can help you calm down." She paused. "If you'll still have me. I'd understand if you don't want to, anymore. Not because of how I look or how I live, but just because I hurt you so badly. The fact you forgive me is huge already. Most people I know would leave forever."

I smirked. "It's a good thing I'm not most people. However, I do think we need to create some ground rules to prevent this from happening again."

"Yes. Like talking to each other more. Being honest when things aren't right."

"Naturally." I shifted so I could lean in and kiss her.

She smiled against my lips. "And I don't want to live here in the castle. I want our own place. I liked having a house. Smaller, sure, but simplicity is much more my style."

Was she saying that she'd stay here? In my world?

"A small house would be perfect," I purred. "Your wish is my command."

"I'm still not sure about this realm…"

"I know, my love." I kissed her again. "We can iron out all the details later. I mean, there's always the possibility of living part of the year here, and part of the year in your world, if we need to. But we have plenty of time to sort things out. Right now, I would much rather make up with you properly."

She blushed, and it was incredibly sexy. "Really? You're feeling that much better?"

We kissed again and a wave of lust rushed over me. I shifted more so she could join me on the bed, but then a sharp pain knifed through my abdomen. "Ah, it seems I'm still tender."

"I'm not going anywhere." She settled into my side and kissed me softly, before adding, "We have plenty of time, my love. We have our whole lives."

Katerina stayed true to her word. She didn't leave my side. She tended to my wounds and helped me recover my lost strength. Slowly but surely, the pain and trauma from my time in the storm healed.

Even though my body craved her during that week together, I enjoyed the time becoming one with her in a different way. We got to know each other on a deeper, more emotionally intimate level, as we both dropped our guard and let the other see the pieces we'd been hiding.

Katerina told me in more detail about the boyfriends who'd lied to her and left.

I, in turn, shared the full truth about what my father had done to my family. Talking healed the wounds of our souls in a way that I'd never thought possible.

"I didn't know that sharing my life with someone would be so freeing," I said to Dymitri as we walked slowly around town one day.

I'd rather have been with Katerina, but I needed my brother's assistance with a special errand.

Dymitri chuckled. "Well, tough guy, I hope this inspires you to let yourself soften around the edges more often."

"I'm ready," I said. "For all of it."

"Including being a father?" Dymitri raised an eyebrow.

"What part of 'for all of it' did you not understand?" I growled playfully.

He held up his hands, laughing some more. "You already have the protective side down. I'm eager to be an uncle and teach your son or daughter all kinds of mischief."

"Whatever you do, you'll get back ten-fold," I said. "Just wait until it's your turn."

"I hope it'll be soon," he said.

A shopkeeper returned with my purchase in a small bag. "It's perfect and polished."

"Thank you." I took the bag and peeked inside at the contents, still in disbelief as to what I had actually just purchased. "Now to return to Katerina."

We made our way back to the castle and found Katerina with Sarah and Nadia in the study. The three sisters sat at a table, hunched forward and talking quietly.

"My love, I don't suppose you'd like to accompany me someplace," I said, reaching a hand out to her and lifting her to her feet.

She smiled up at me. "I think I'd love that. I wanted to talk to you anyway about something important."

How convenient. "Let's go."

Slowly, she settled her hand more comfortably in my grip. I couldn't help reaching out to run my other hand over her burgeoning belly. Our baby was growing fast.

She waved goodbye to her sisters, and then we left the castle. I led her right to the edge of town and beyond, almost to the edge of my brother's kingdom. We strolled through the outlying streets, where it was quieter than the busy center of town where the castle was situated, and I made sure to give her ample time to absorb our peaceful surroundings.

"This is beautiful," she said, after a time. "Quiet and so cute!"

"I thought you'd enjoy it out here," I said. "Away from the busiest parts of the kingdom. We have one last place to visit."

I brought her to the end of the street we were in, where an iron gate stood blocking the rest of the path. I pulled a large key from my pocket and unlocked the gate. Then I led Katerina down the path. The town faded from view behind a small forest of trees.

"All day, I've been wanting to show you this," I said. We finally came up to an empty plot of land. "I haven't made any official decision yet because I wanted to make sure you liked this spot."

"For?" she asked, gazing around. "I'm not sure I understand."

"For a house."

Her eyes widened as she gazed up at me. "A house? You mean…"

"Yes. For us. I want to build a home here for us. I know how much you dislike the idea of living in the castle. This felt like the perfect place to make something of our own." My heart began to pound hard in my chest. I couldn't remember the last time I'd ever felt this nervous. "If you'd like to, that is?"

Katerina continued to gaze up at me. She was smiling, so that had to be a good sign. "You want to build a house from scratch?"

"Yes."

"All by yourself?"

"I might need a little help," I said with a smirk. "But you shouldn't doubt my skills after what I did to your home back in the other realm."

She laughed. "Good point."

"We can design it together," I continued. "Make plans and…" I swallowed. "I would love to do this as your husband."

"Yeah, I can see it now. We can…" She then stopped and her brow knit together. "Wait… what? Did you say…"

There was no taking it back now. "I want you to be my wife. Katerina, will you marry me?" I reached into my pocket and pulled out the simple yet elegant ring I'd purchased in town earlier with Dymitri.

I slowly got down on one knee in front of her. Her hands rose to her mouth and her eyes were like saucers as she stared at me.

"You're all I've ever dreamed of, and I would be the luckiest man alive to call you my wife. I'm already so fortunate that we're starting a family. Let's make this dream official."

She let out a shocked-sounding gasp, and then quickly followed with a chuckle. "I… Lucian… of course! Yes, yes, I'll marry you!"

She suddenly rushed forward and wrapped her arms around

my shoulders before leaning down to kiss me. I got to my feet and kissed her back, not holding in any of my passion. I lifted her into my arms and carried her over to a blanket I'd already spread out over the grass when I visited here earlier. The goal had been to recreate the picnic she made for me the day she told me of her pregnancy.

Katerina picked up on it right away. "You remembered every detail." She gasped. "Even the color of the blanket."

"I remember everything you do," I admitted. I set her down carefully then joined her. "Especially something so kind."

Tears pooled in her eyes, and she kissed me. "Never leave me again, okay? Even if I say something stupid, I can't stand the thought of you not being in my life. It would devastate me."

"As you wish." I crushed my mouth to hers again, hungry and desperate to show her the depth of my love.

It was summer in my realm, and although it was still cool, this unusually warm day made my plans to seduce her very possible.

Words were not always easy for me, but actions? With those, I could get my message across. The dragon inside of me was burning for his mate, and I couldn't agree more. We'd waited long enough.

I put my hand up her skirt and pulled down her panties, pleased to feel her wetness against my fingers as I did so. Then I ripped open my pants. She helped release my cock from its confines and then climbed on top of me. There was no time for finesse. We had gone without for far too long.

I let out a quiet growl as I guided her down onto the fullness of my cock, impaling her fully. She let out a soft whimper of pleasure.

I cupped her full breasts through the material of her bra and enjoyed the feel of her warm body, her luscious curves, and her hot, wet channel tight around my flesh. Her fingers dug into my chest, and mine swept over her waist, her swollen belly and down to tease her clit as she rode me.

She moaned against my lips as she leaned down and kissed me. I cherished every touch. I pulled off her blouse and freed her breasts from her bra.

We loved one another until we were spent.

I panted, breathless and tried to keep her connected to me for as long as possible. She slowly, reluctantly, rolled off and lay down beside me.

"I've missed you," I said. "The taste of you. The feel of you. The little sounds you make when your desire ratchets up."

"Now I feel like we've officially made up," she said with a sigh. "Is that weird?"

"Not at all." I felt exactly the same way.

She kissed my nose and eventually stood to find and gather all her pieces of clothing that we'd scattered in our haste. She carefully dressed and adjusted her blouse to cover those luscious breasts, much to my disappointment. "Lucian," she said when she lay down beside me again. "I had something I wanted to talk to you about."

"Ah, yes, you did mention that earlier," I said as I rolled onto my side to face her.

"Yes, and you successfully distracted me from it! At least for a little while." She giggled, then her expression turned serious, and I couldn't help but worry. Katerina cleared her throat. "When I was at the doctor, they took a lot of pictures of the baby. They also were able to find out the sex."

My eyes lit up at the idea. "And?"

"I haven't actually looked," she said.

"Oh. What stopped you?" I asked. Surely, she would want to know if she was having a boy, or a girl?

"After you told me how hurt you were for not being involved, I decided it should be something we either do together, or not at all." My heart sped up. She wanted to wait and do this with me?

A huge grin spread across my face, and she cupped my cheek, smiling back at me for a moment, before she turned away and reached over for her purse. She pulled out an envelope. "What do you think? Should we find out? Or be surprised?"

I put my hand over hers and we held the envelope together. "This is a tough choice, Kat. It'd be like opening a birthday present early. On the other hand… I'm not known for my patience."

"So, we're going to look?" she asked, her eyes lighting up with pleasure.

It was obvious what her choice was, so I grinned at her again. "We are definitely going to look!"

"Okay. On three?"

"All right. One." I gazed into her eyes, seeing the love she was no longer trying to hide.

"Two." She smiled the brightest of smiles and my heart did a funny flip-flop.

"Three," I half-shouted, and together, weripped the envelope open.

EPILOGUE

Twelve months later
Lucian

I sawed a piece of wood in half and added it to my pile in the backyard. Once again, I was working on building a deck for my beautiful wife. I was using the same design from her old house. She'd loved that one a lot, and I wanted to make our new home feel like one for her just as much as myself. So far, progress seemed to be going well.

In nine months, I'd been able to build the actual house. We'd made sure the blueprints included five bedrooms. One for us, at least three future children, and a guest room. There was also space on the land to create a guesthouse on the property, and that was next on my list once I finished landscaping the yard around the main house.

Katerina's dad wasn't well, and we had decided, after talking to Sarah and Nadia as well, that we should bring him here to live with us. He would have the guest house on our property for as long as he wanted it. And Katerina would have the pleasure of her father not too far away.

But first, I needed to finish this deck, and then I'd build the best of treehouse playgrounds for our active child. Katerina insisted that could wait until later. Babies couldn't climb trees, after all.

I suppose she was right, but I couldn't help it. I wanted whatever children we had to have everything. Spoiling Katerina and our beautiful son gave me the greatest of joys.

The sound of crying burst out of the windows from the top floor, my hearing picking up the moment my son was awake. I set down my tools and left the backyard for the nursery. I walked upstairs and quietly entered the room.

"Victor, you're awake just in time. Mommy will be home soon from work," I said.

He stood up on his little chubby legs, gripping the side of the crib I'd made him. One hand reached out to me. "Dadadada!"

"Yes, I'm here." I picked up my beautiful son and held him close.

I'd been so worried about becoming a father. I'd thought it wouldn't come naturally to me, and I'd struggle with learning how to love Victor properly. Taking care of his basic needs was never the concern. Just loving him, and learning how to love him in a way that didn't damage him. Like my father had done to me and Dymitri.

But from the moment he'd been born, it all fell into place. I held him for the first time and knew instantly that loving Victor would never be a problem. Much like loving Katerina had been as easy as breathing, the love for our son Victor came just as naturally.

After I'd proposed, and we'd told everyone here at the castle our exciting news, we flew back to Katerina's house in the human realm, and began our plans to settle down. Katerina wanted to finish the school year with her students, so we lived in her house until the summer. It was different this time, though, because things were good between my mate and me, and we had made the decision to return to live in my realm.

My dragon was sated by that news and remained quiet and content. At least, as quiet and content as it is possible for a dragon to be.

During that time, we got the place ready to sell and moved our things to the castle, all while planning a wedding.

The ceremony was simple yet elegant. We married on our property and honeymooned in the new house I built. Katerina spoke to Damon about teaching at the small school in town, for which he gave his grateful permission, and then she gave birth in the middle of summer.

Victor was now seven months old, and he'd just started standing with a little help. Watching him hit each milestone in development continued to blow my mind. I couldn't believe how smart he was, or how adorable. Watching him while Katerina worked at the school was not hard at all.

For the time being, my job was to keep working on the house, which I primarily did on the weekends and for a few hours after Katerina came home from work. Some small projects I did during Victor's nap time. When our house was finished, the plan was for me to expand my love of construction into a business.

There was so much to rebuild still in this kingdom—a legacy of my father's tyranny, but for the first time, I felt excited about the opportunities for building rather than angry at the previous destruction he'd caused.

We were close to my family, and also to hers. I flew her home to visit her father and her old school whenever she wanted, and of course, once our guesthouse was ready, he would come to live with us permanently. For now, he was happy with occasional visits. Sarah and Nadia loved to come over and babysit their nephew as well.

In our house in the forest, Katerina and I were finally able to be ourselves. In doing so, we saw how truly compatible we were with one another. She liked my quiet, strong, rough exterior, yet also appreciated my softer, hidden side. She didn't mind that I acted grumpy. My personality gave her a calm and safe place to hide when the world sometimes became too overwhelming.

In turn, I loved Katerina's boldness and newfound self-confidence. She didn't have any issues stating her opinions, and she wasn't afraid of putting me in my place when needed. There was a tender, nurturing side to her as well that left me never doubting if she loved me. Even when she was mad, I could still sense her love underlying it. A constant reassurance that everything would be all right.

For the first time in our lives, we both had balance. Katerina had her dream job and retained access to the world she loved. I had the freedom of letting my dragon fly and performing my duties for the realm. Life might not have been perfect, but we had gotten pretty damn close to it. Even if a situation rocked the boat in the future, I didn't worry about us capsizing in the storm. We'd sail through, stronger in the end. I could feel it in my soul.

The knob turned for the front door.

"Mamamama!" Victor squealed with delight.

"Yes! Mommy's home!" I made my way to greet her in the foyer. The moment she saw us, she shot me a huge smile and automatically reached for Victor.

"Hey, baby," she cooed and cuddled him close to her. He squealed and touched her face with his tiny hands. The way she smiled down at him with so much adoration and love... It was my favorite expression of hers.

I leaned in and kissed her lips. "How was school today?"

"Excellent. All the students are making me feel like a valued part of the community," she said. "Which is awesome and kind of a surprise since I'm pretty new here. They treat me like I've been around for a while."

"I knew you'd fit in perfectly."

A fact that relieved me, because I'd been nervous. Everything about my realm was new and mysterious to Katerina. She'd expressed so much hesitation when we first met. Since she had embraced my dragon, she also seemed to have fully embraced living in my world. I'd thought she might resent me, but I quickly learned Katerina was a woman of her word. If she said she was willing to go all in, she meant it.

And she went all in with me.

"I've been asked to help plan the next family event at the school," she said. "I can't wait to show you my classroom and introduce you to my students. A lot of them know of you but not much about you, so they ask me all sorts of questions."

I chuckled. "They'll be stunned when they see how normal and boring I am, compared to my brothers."

"It'll do great things for the kingdom, though." She smiled up at me, and I appreciated her thinking about that bigger-picture aspect of our life.

Regardless of whether or not I was a legitimate heir to the throne, my brother, Damon, had a lot of damage to undo. I'd be a willing part of that.

"What did you do today?" she asked.

"Worked outside," I said. "Victor did a lot of swinging while I got the planks ready for the new deck. It should be finished within a few days."

"A few days? Wow, you're a machine." She shook her head.

I winked. "Not only in the bedroom."

"Are you sure you're human?" she teased. "I mean, I know

you're a dragon, but what about a robot? Are there mechanical dragons?"

"You know I'm all flesh," I growled playfully. "Or do I need to remind you later?"

She pretended to think. "Gosh, my memory is awfully foggy."

"Mama!" Victor interrupted.

"Oh, sorry. Are we traumatizing you with our love?" She bopped Victor's nose. "And do you help Daddy while he works outside?"

"He does by talking to me. I'm not sure what he was saying today, but he had a lot of opinions about it."

"Dada do," Victor said, lifting up his hands.

"Yes, Daddy does work hard," she said.

I gave her a weak smile. "He just woke up from his nap. I know, it's later than usual. I was so sucked into my work."

"Guess we'll have a later night," she said. "He's growing, so he's probably extra tired."

She brought him into the kitchen, and I loved how she made him a part of everything she did. Victor couldn't help by any means, but she talked him through her day and the process of whatever task she was completing. Whenever I wondered what I should do, I looked to Katerina as a guide.

From the moment I found out we were having a son, I knew it was an opportunity to break the cycle my father had continued. I had a choice: follow in his damaging footsteps or pave my own way and try to do it right. Doing my own thing wasn't as difficult as I thought with Katerina to help guide me and be by my side through everything. She was a teacher at heart, after all, and excellent at her job.

I was going to do far better as a father than I'd ever dreamed of, and Victor was going to grow up to be an amazing young man because of it. Together, Katerina and I would start a new legacy.

I watched my wife with my son and couldn't hold in the joy. I released a shout of laughter, and they looked over at me and both of them began to chuckle.

Our life was simple—beautiful. I couldn't ask for anything more. Love had won, and I had my heart's desire right here in front of me in the smiling faces of my loving wife and happy child.

THE END

The next book in the series, **The Human Mate for the Dragon Prince,** will be available in early 2022.

You can pre-order:
https://books2read.com/u/bQjBEZ

Or read on for a sneak peek:

ONE

Anselm.

My parent's romance was legendary. It was whispered about by the townspeople, and their disgusting habit of feeling each other up in public was enough to make my sisters and I puke.

"Can you tell them to tone it down?" My sister Victoria whispered at me, rolling her eyes.

I groaned and straightened up where I stood waiting for our parents to look up. We were in the most private living room in the castle, with a roaring fire in the grate and luxurious textures on the furniture and walls.

Then, when they continued to canoodle on the couch, I cleared my throat loudly. "Mother. Father."

They turned around to stare at us, as if they hadn't known we were there the whole time.

My father, King Stavrok, raised an eyebrow. "Oh, Anselm. Vicki. Can we help you?"

"Yes. We wanted to speak to you for a moment." I said, stepping forward.

"Of course, sweetheart. Have a seat." Our mother said.

Our mom, Lucy, was human, and didn't possess the formality that was required of the royal line.

She loved us though. And that was all that mattered, according to our father.

I sat on the couch opposite our parents and Victoria perched nearby.

"Vicky?" Mom asked. "What's up?"

Victoria dove straight to the core of the issue. "Anselm and I would like to ask permission to go away for the summer."

Our sister, Toni, was living with her husband Prince Viktor, at his parent's castle to the south. She was expecting her first baby already, and according to her mother in law Marienne, they were twin boys.

Toni had a life. We didn't and we wanted to change that.

Mom and Dad glanced at each other as though they were surprised to hear it.

I slid back on the couch and crossed my ankle over my knee. "It's time we left the castle."

My Dad grinned at me. "Living in poverty are you?"

I rolled my eyes at him. "No, of course not."

At twenty-three I felt like a pampered prince. I'd had the best of everything, my whole twenty-three years of life. Good family. Support. Love.

I knew I was lucky. But there was something gnawing at me to get out and see the world.

"Then what is it, honey?" Mom asked. "I'm sure Damon and Cass would love to see you if you want to see the North. They can always use the help. Even twenty years later, they're still rebuilding that kingdom."

I shook my head. "Thanks Mom, but I'd rather do something different."

"I'll go visit Auntie Cass!" Vicky said. "It's been too long since I've seen them, and I know they're always up for some help with their kids."

Dad chuckled. "Hell yes they are. Especially with Dymitri and Lucian's kids being raised in the castle also. I thought you triplets were a handful, but you'll have ten dragon shifters to contend with if you go as a baby sitter, Vicky."

She shrugged. "I'd love it. At least for a couple of weeks. It'll be a nice change of pace."

Vicky had a natural maternal urge that I didn't share. Especially since I'd almost been set up fire by Lucian's youngest son last time I was there.

The royal families of fire and ice had expanded exponentially.

"Of course, you can, Vicky." Dad said. "I'll fly up with you if you want to go tomorrow?"

Then he glanced at mum. "Would you like to come? It's been a while since you visited."

Mum smiled. "I'd love to. Let's all go."

I shook my head. "No... I'd like to go somewhere else for the summer."

"Like where?"

I didn't really want to tell them, but the compulsion to tell my parents the truth was always strong. I took a breath and told them the truth.

"I want to go to the human world and find my mate."

Pre-order link:
https://books2read.com/u/bQjBEZ